Lords of the Afterglow
Renegades and Noblemen

More Adventurous Mayhem from
Santiago and Johnny Rico

by
Judge Santiago Burdon

Lords of the Afterglow

Renegades and Noblemen

More Adventurous Mayhem from Santiago and Johnny Rico

by Judge Santiago Burdon

Lords of the Afterglow

By Judge Santiago Burdon

First Edition

Author: Judge Santiago Burdon
Editor: Paul Gilliland
Formatting: Southern Arizona Press
Cover Artwork: Zain Ali – Pexels.com

Published by Southern Arizona Press
Sierra Vista, Arizona 85635
www.SouthernArizonaPress.com

ISBN: 978-1-960038-24-1

Short Stories

Dedication

Dennis *'Saint Alfonso'* Veeder

Contents

The Twice Killed Cat   8

Johnny Rico and El Oso Rojo   16

Luck of the I Wish   24

Get Forked   29

Mickey Sixpence   36

Los Dos Chiflados [Two Wacky Guys]   42

Do You Ever Think About Me   52

Psychopath Merit Badge   56

Who Doesn't Like Strawberries   60

The Bare Necessities   68

Lavatory Lockup   82

God Might Be a Woman   93

Johnny's Junk in the Truck   118

Peyote, Toads, and the Medicine Man   137

No Boats   153

Where in the World is Johnny Rico   164

Acknowledgments   183

About the Author   184

Previous Works   185

The Twice Killed Cat

We became acquainted in a Mexican prison, where I was a guest for eight months. I made it a policy to never associate with people I'd met in prison once I was back on the outside, but in Johnny Rico's case, he was the exception to the rule. Sort of like a mild virus you're unable to shake. You know you're infected, but you just learn to live with the malady. Always with a bandanna around his neck and most of the time its color clashed with his shirt. He says it serves as a fashion statement, but I've never been able to figure out what exactly he statement he was trying to say. Then there's his common practice of always wearing mismatched socks all the time. I'm sure he's colorblind and I've tried to demonstrate the fact with simple a test numerous times, but he'll never have any part of my experiment. He's very egocentric and will never admit to making a mistake or having a disability, but he's my carnal [a Mexican slang word for a friend who is like family] and has always been there for me. My proverbial Colombian guardian angel.

I gave him the last name Rico, which fits his personality hand in glove. Commonly translated as "rich" or "wealthy", it can also mean exceptional, and for better or worse, that is Johnny all the way.

Cartagena, Columbia - A place so beautiful that even God couldn't believe he'd created it with his own hands. If he vacations, I have no doubt this is his destination. Gorgeous women, true angeles sin alas, obras de arte [angels without wings, works of art]. If God created a woman more beautiful than these Colombianas, he must have kept her up in heaven for himself. Cartagena also happens to be the hometown of my lunatic sidekick, Johnny Rico.

There I am relaxing by the pool, working up an appetite for dinner with twelve-ounce curls, letting the sun have its way with me while recuperating from the night before. "Excuse me, Mr. Bigote [whiskers, specifically moustache],” says Raul, the concierge. “There's a call for you. Would you like for me to bring the phone poolside?”

I'd made a request that I was not to be disturbed, interrupted, or bothered in any way, but I guess the call must be important enough to disregard my request. “Do you know who it is?” I ask. “No, Mister Bigotes, but he said it was an emergency.” That's all I needed to hear; instantly the mystery was solved. “I'll take the call on the phone in the lobby.”

I reached into my wallet and gave him a healthy propina [tip], informing him that he never took this call for me. He nods to indicate his understanding.

“Diga me! Quien es?” says the voice on the other line. “Bigotes, I am very sorry to bother you ...” Which of course, he was not. “It's Johnny,” he says. “I have a big problem, and I really need your help!”

At first, I can only detect a faint quiver in his voice. Then, all at once, he starts crying uncontrollably. In all the time I'd known the man, I'd never known him to cry, and we had seen enough shit together that would have warranted it.

“Okay Johnny, find some huevos and meet me for dinner at Tesoro del Mar, 7:30 sharp. Entiendas pinche?”

“Okay Bigotes, gracias carnal.”

“Don't thank me yet.”

Later, at the restaurant, I wind up dining alone. Wiping my mouth, I take a look at my watch. 8:15 pm. I swear, Colombians are more proficient at tardiness than even Mexicans. It's a common and even accepted practice in this country to be late.

Just as I'm about to pay the check for my dinner and wine, in strolls Rico, looking as though his dog had just been run over.

"Did you order dinner already?" he asks dejectedly.

"Not only did I already order dinner, JR. I ate dinner, drank a bottle of wine, and tipped the bartender, the cook, and the waiter. Now I am on the prowl for some of Colombia's finest cocaine, an angel of the evening, and an orgy of such depravity and lewdness it would make a porn star blush. A night I won't remember. Are ya in, carnal?"

"I thought you were buying me dinner?" he whines. "That was at 7:30. It is now close to 8:30."

"Are you going to start with that 'gringo time' again, carnal?"

"Okay," I relent. "Have a seat, I'll buy ya dinner. Como pasando contigo? Que haces dime?" [What's going on with you? What are you doing?]

He begins to regale me with the tragedy that has caused him so much pain of late. His lower lip quavers and his hands begin to tremble as he speaks. From the way he is acting, I'm sure he has either fucked up big time or fucked somebody over, earning him a spot on their list.

"She's cheating on me with some cabrón at work!" he finally blurts out. "She's fucking someone else, I'm sure of it. My heart has been killed twice!"

"Son of a bitch," I thought, "it's about a woman this time instead." This coming from a guy who would fuck a bush if he thought a snake was in it. Over dinner, I note that his heartbreak sure hasn't affected his appetite. Two plates of pescado frito, arroz, salada, sopa, and cuatro cervezas later, we are finally ready to commence this mission of restoring my carnal's manhood. As we exit the restaurant, Johnny is still talking rapidly, crying, his hands flailing in the air.

"Johnny, shut the fuck up," I eventually tell him. "So, what's this master plan?" I have participated in enough of his adventures in the past, some of which would make a schizophrenic's actions seem normal. We reach his car and I slide in the passenger side, immediately noticing the odd assortment of items in back. Bottles of tequila, beer (undoubtedly warm), rope, flashlights, and what looks like a box trap of some kind. It's similar to what my grandma used to catch raccoons in her attic. Why I'm even entertaining the thought of assisting this lunatic in whatever he has in mind this time is far beyond me. It is in this moment I have to admit, Johnny Rico, insane though he may be, is my friend. That's a word I have never used lightly, and while my standards of friendship are extremely high, I reciprocate by the same set of standards. In other words, guess I'm in.

"First, we are to stake out her house," he begins at length. "Then, we will wait for her cat to come along and trap it. Then, we are going to stab that son of a bitch until it's dead TWICE and hang it from her door. When she comes home and sees it, she will know that no one disrespects Juan Villanova Johnny Rico and gets away with it!" Johnny always had to kill something twice. I'd never understood where that ritual originated from, and I'd never thought to ask until now.

"Uh huh ..." I say. "So, you think the best way to win her back is by mutilating her cat, killing it twice, and hanging it from her door. What is this, some sort of Santa Muerta ritual, or an ancient Indian ritual kinda thing?"

"No, this is all my idea," he confesses proudly. "I thought of it myself!" Like I never would have guessed.

It is then that Johnny pulls out a bag of cocaine the size of his fist, gleefully shoving it in my face. It's not like he has to force me to partake. I open the bag and snort a healthy amount through his silver coke straw and he does the same. I pop open a warm beer for me and one for my carnal, take a large hit of tequila, and pass the bottle over to Johnny. Together we speed off into the night.

It is 9:20 pm when we run out of gas three blocks from his girlfriend's house. We have to walk two kilometers to a gas station, through a barrio I was not very comfortable strolling about in at night. Johnny, meanwhile, seems oblivious to the danger, trudging ever onward without fear. He assures me he has earned safe passage through almost every neighborhood in the city. I doubt his dispensation but don't express my disbelief. Finally, we return to the car and gas it back up. Slowly we creep down Johnny's girlfriend's street, lights off, but for some reason he has got the radio blaring.

"Johnny, the radio!" I yell, "Turn it off, pendejo!"

"Si, si," he complies, "I don't like this song either ..." For Christ's sake, if he's going for stealth, it's a lost cause already.

He parks the car across the street, in an alleyway with a perfect view of her house.

"I see that you've done this before," I observe. "How long have you been stalking her, JR? This is not a healthy activity, carnal."

"Only four or five times," he confesses. "How else to make sure she's not fucking around on me?"

Stepping out of the car, we quickly get the trap set up and Johnny puts an unopened carton of milk inside.

"Johnny," I laugh, "that's never gonna work! Have you got any fish, maybe a can of tuna or something?"

"No, but that's a good idea," he says. "Come on, let's go get a can of tuna..."

Half an hour later, we return with the tuna, bait the trap, and resume our surveillance mission.

"You know Rico, wouldn't it have been easier to just send her a box of dog shit, like you did to that prostitute you were so madly in love with? What was her name? 'Laura the Zorra [slut], if I remember correctly?"

"First of all, Bigotes, she wasn't a prostitute! That was a rumor started by some bitches, chismosas [gossipy women], only because they were jealous of her. So don't you call her a zorra! Also, that pinche gato got into my Toyota and pissed all over inside. I could never get the smell out and had to sell the car for pennies, do you remember? So, the gato deserves what he has coming to him!"

"Isn't that the car you sold your sister? And Johnny, with all due respect to working girls, she was a prostitute whether you want to believe it or not!"

"Ya, yo, se carnal, I know she was a prostitute. And my sister never did figure out what that smell was, either!"

I start laughing uncontrollably and Johnny joins in, unable to catch his breath. There's snot running from my nose, and the sight of it sends Johnny into complete hysterics. There we sat laughing, smoking cigarettes and joints, drinking beer and tequila and snorting cocaine well into the night. We're telling jokes, lies about women we've had, and exchanging stories of close calls experienced on dope runs. All the while waiting on a cat that may or may not decide to show up.

Two hours later and it's close to midnight. My speech has become so slurred, it is practically incomprehensible. I'm talking fast without punctuation, Chicago style, speaking total Cocainese. I could run a marathon with a beer in one hand and a joint in the other, with Johnny on my back, I am so coked up by this point. It is then I look outside the window, noticing the mountain of beer cans and cigarette butts that has accumulated on the ground beside the car. That's when it occurs to me how bad I need to piss. Opening the door, I stumble out over the mess, and Johnny follows suit.

"Bigotes, mira playo [there's her cat]!" he says, before I can even get unzipped. "Venga gatito, venga bebe ..." The cat walks right up to Johnny and start rubbing against his leg. What happens next isn't pretty. I immediately grab the bottle of tequila, guzzling a monstrous amount. "Now, I kill this fucking cat twice!" he screams, raising his knife yet again.

"Johnny, that's enough!" I almost can't believe the sheer level of the brutality I've just witnessed. I never thought he'd actually go through with it. I nearly double over and start puking right then and there, but somehow I manage to maintain my composure.

Next thing I know, we're standing on his girlfriend's porch. Grinning maniacally, Johnny does the deed as promised, tying the poor creature's carcass to her door.

"Okay," I say, "let's get the fuck out of here!"

"What!? No carnal, I want to see her reaction ..."

My friend has proven himself to be a total psychopath, but I am far too tired, shocked, and fucked up by this point to offer much by way of resistance. Johnny hands me a joint. I light it, take a hit, cough, and follow him back to the car. He hasn't even attempted to clean the blood off himself. It is now close to dawn, and soon the sun will be shedding its light on Johnny's heinous crimes, to which I have become an unwitting accomplice.

It isn't long before a car pulls up to his girlfriend's house. She climbs out and Johnny smiles wide, poking me in the ribs to make sure I'm still awake. He wants us both to see what happens next.

Meanwhile, an old woman is sweeping the sidewalk in front of the house next door. She looks up as a scream pierces the stillness of the morning. Abruptly dropping her broom, she hurries over to where Johnny's girlfriend stands screaming on her porch.

"My cat, my cat!" the old woman begins to shriek. "My baby! Oh, my poor Tito ..."

Johnny just stares straight ahead with a blank expression on his face.

"Wrong cat," he says.

Johnny Rico And El Oso Rojo

There's a persistent knock at my door. I should characterize it as more of a pounding than a knock. It's 2:19 a.m. and I don't have to guess who would be so rude, so impatient as to disrupt and disturb me at this hour. I'm sure of the identity of the intruder and he must be off his meds. I open the door without asking the person outside to identify himself.

"Oh, good Bigotes, you are awake. I hope I'm not interrupting anything? Listen, I need your help to get revenge on the Jamaicans that ripped me off last month. I know where they are staying. Can you come with me now?" Johnny Rico asks while pushing his way into my apartment.

Johnny has been a friend for nine years now. We're partners in the import-export business. I'm sure he's clinically insane but has always watched my back and is the only person I trust in the world.

"Ya got any beer?" He says as he makes his way to the refrigerator.

"Are you for real? It's almost 2:30 in the morning and you want me to head out on some revenge-capade to get back at some Jamaicans for a couple hundred dollars? Are you insane? Of course, you are, what a ludicrous question," I holler.

"So, what do you say Bigotes?" He inquires.

"Hold on, let me get some clothes on and do a bump!" I surrender.

I keep asking myself over and over what possesses me to become an active participant in these deranged and demented acts of psychosis? I've never been able to find an answer.

"Hey, carnal, grab your Glock. Just in case things get out of control. Ya know, some insurance."

"Hey J.R., I'm really starting to not enjoy this scenario. Guns? What are you planning to accomplish? And I want a rational answer. No off the wall psycho babble." I say in a stern voice. I can see in his eyes that he's riding The Bi-Polar Express.

"I just want those Caribbean Chulos [pimps] to know who they're dealing with. They can't come to Colombia, my country and disrespect me. These Rastamen need to learn a lesson," Johnny screams.

"So now you're a teacher giving lessons? In what, 'Johnny's brand of street justice?' Listen I will accompany you on this mission of restoring your pride, but no killing anything twice. Do you understand?"

"I don't want it to come to that, but if it happens, I gotta do what I got to do. Now let's go! They have a house in Barrio Los Lomas."

I cautiously climb into Oso Rojo [red bear], a monstrous automobile, and am swallowed up by the plush seat. Johnny bought this 1974 Buick LeSabre from some corrupt Federal Police at an incredibly discounted price. It's blood red with a white convertible top. You'd have a difficult time going unnoticed in this oversized pimpmobile. He had a Dodge Duster prior to this impulsive purchase which wasn't as high profile and drew very little attention. The Duster became a victim of one of Johnny's psychotic episodes, after a three-day cocaine binge, accompanied by a case of Scotch and an array of prescription medications he pilfered from the last psychiatric hospital where he resided for a week. They demanded he leave. They'd had enough of his "Riconess." He drove the Duster into a concrete retaining wall near the beach. Then in a bizarre ritual to some ancient god, he set the car on fire. The Duster was beyond restoration and never did rise from the ashes. There was no resurrecting the Duster. He left it right there in the middle of the highway and never looked back.

"So carnal, what's the plan? You have some idea of how you're going to address this offensive? I mean what is your strategy?" I ask.

"I didn't think about it. I thought I would leave it up to you. You are so good at figuring out how to attack a problem."

We arrive at the house where the suspects reside and surprisingly, they're still awake. We can see them partying inside through some large sliding glass doors . The music is blaring and you can hear them laughing, talking, and dancing around.

"What the hell is that music they are listening to? That's not ABBA is it? Is that ABBA? You said these were Rastamen. Big bad Rastamen set me up and ripped me off Bigotes. That's what you told me." I say imitating a whimpering child. "RICO! Where's their dreadlocks and Bob Marley Reggae Music Mon? No self-respecting Rastafarian would be listening to ABBA! Ya know what I think, Johnny Rico? I surmise you met these Cabrons at that Gay Disco Club in downtown Cartagena and attempted to rip them off. That's exactly what happened isn't it? They got the drop on you," I tease.

"Callate cabron! That's not what happened. You know I'm not gay. I go to the club for the music. It doesn't matter how it went down. Those pinches stole my money, my coca, and my watch. You're making me angry, Bigotes. You better stop making fun of me. Thought you're my friend, my carnal?" He says.

He's irritated and truly upset. Johnny isn't one for practical jokes or being the subject of ridicule.

"Well, how are we going to lure them outside? It's not like they're going to offer us an invitation to come inside for a cocktail," I say while chuckling.

"Think it's still funny? I've got a way to get inside. Hold on Bigotes!" Johnny hollers.

He doesn't answer my question as how we're going to enter the house. Instead, Johnny backs up the Monstrous Red Road Schooner, revs the engine, slams the shifter into drive and with tires squealing we head toward the arcadia glass doors at an accelerated velocity.

"Johnny you psychopath! You're going to kill both of us!" I yelp in a high-pitched scream.

"Invitation? We don't need no stinking invitation, carnal!" He yells.

Within seconds the Red Road Schooner, becomes a Transformer and morphs into a tank then makes impact with the door and section of the block wall. I watch the Jamaicans scurry out of the way into safety. The sound of glass shattering and furniture being demolished echoes loudly and takes me to a fever pitch. Johnny slams on the brakes and the Oso Rojo stops short of the wall on the other side of the room.

"Come on, Bigotes!" Johnny yells.

He pulls out his antique .38 police special revolver and starts firing off rounds toward the room where the Jamaicans have taken refuge. In all the years I've known my lunatic sidekick, I've never seen him shoot that pistol.

"Bigotes, cover me!" He commands.

The *Mamma Mia* soundtrack accompanies us still playing on the stereo adding to the already surreal atmosphere. Here we go again. My gun has found my hand and I squeeze off a few rounds. I take aim at the stereo and kill the damn thing. The music was agitating the hell out of me.

"I hate ABBA!" I scream.

Johnny is yelling insults in Spanish demanding the Jamaicans show themselves. They begin throwing out money along with a couple of watches. I shoot at a large mirror that almost covers the entire wall. Simply because I had nothing else to do. Pieces come crashing down on top of Johnny where he's crawling crablike on the floor picking up the cash and watches.

"Cabron que haces pendejo?" He grabs a brass lamp and returns to the car. We jump inside the enormous automobile covered with glass and drywall debris. I fire off a couple of more rounds at a picture of women with baskets of tropical fruit on their heads.

"Let's get the hell outta here Rico."

"Wait, I want something."

"Johnny whatcha doing? Come on venga," I plead.

He exits Oso Rojo and runs to a picture hanging on the far wall. It's one of those grotesque velvet paintings of Marilyn Monroe or possibly Madonna. He shoves the ugly painting in the back seat, breaking the wooden frame. The car has been idling the entire time and the room is filled with exhaust making it difficult to breathe.

"Johnny Rico has left the building!" He screams.

Then he grinds the shifter into reverse and the mighty big car pulls out crushing whatever rubble we created during our entrance. I notice Johnny's face and arms are bleeding caused by pieces of the mirror I destroyed and landed on top of him. He stops the Red Bear on the street and we get out to clean the remains of wreckage laying on the hood and roof. I see neighbors on their porches and watching out their windows. I smile and wave at the spectators.

"Those are very bad people. They molested my cousin and she's only ten years old," I tell the crowd in Spanish.

Some folks start applauding our dirty deed. An old man yells out, "We didn't see or hear anything. God bless you."

We jump back in the Red Beast and head back toward my apartment.

"Hey Rico, whatcha say we put the top down, grab some beers, park at the beach, and watch the sunrise. Sound like a plan?" I suggest.

"What did I say earlier? You always know how to make times better. You have the perfect idea. Ya carnal, let's do that."

We reach the beach and sit in the Red Whale not saying a word.

"I love you carnal. You are more than family," Johnny declares, breaking the silence.

"Ya, I know man. I know."

"I haven't counted the plata," Johnny whispers.

He plunges his hand into his pocket and produces a wad of bills and throws it on the console between the seats. He puts his hand in the other front pocket and again a fistful of bills appears.

"Hijo de puta! Look Bigotes, we got a lot back," he says giggling like a child. When he finishes counting the booty he lets out a yell that I'm sure could be heard in Bogota.

"There's over $1,700," he declares.

"That's in Colombian pesos J.R. It converts into what, about twenty-three dollars in American money," I comment sarcastically.

"No carnal that is in American money after doing the change," he says.

"Here, Hermano, take some. You helped me in one of my crazy schemes again. You are always there for me when I need a friend. Here tome, I want you to have this!"

I accepted his generous offering and later discovered he gave me over seven hundred dollars. "Thanks carnal, I appreciate your generosity. A toast to a friendship made to last long after forever," I proclaim. Our beer cans clank to the declaration of friendship toast.

"Hey Bigotes, take the lamp too. It would look good in your home. I think maybe in your bedroom to replace that ugly lamp with all the flowers; and a watch for you and a watch for me. A reminder of our adventure in the Big Red Bear," Johnny says proudly.

"Thanks, carnal, I'm just relieved we made it out alive, ya lunatic." I look closely at the watch and notice it's a Louis Moinet an incredibly expensive time piece. I strap it on my wrist and stare at the second hand ticking my life away.

And there we stayed until the sun had bled every bit of crimson colored light into the morning. Two displaced souls searching for directions to a destination that neither weas sure existed. *Here Comes the Sun* plays on the radio.

"Hey Johnny, I want you to know something."

"What do you want me to know?"

"I am never going out with you again."

In case you were wondering, that grotesque velvet painting? Madonna!

Luck of the 'I' Wish

Our small plane is being tossed around by the wind's unforgiving fury accompanied by a rain that's pummeling the Beech Bonanza. We're a paper bag in a tornado, at the mercy of its chaotic force. Our pilot, Salinas, also known by Demonio Mosca [demon fly], appears unaffected by the storm. The deluge is pelting the windshield, with only a single wiper swaying lazily, making it almost impossible to see. Guess it doesn't matter, all there is to view are black clouds in a dark sky anyway. Salinas can only see half of what is going on due to the fact he only has one eye.

Johnny Rico is screaming from in back cursing the rocking motion. It's causing his beer to spill. We're on a course to imminent disaster, it's a flight plan straight to hell and he's worried about a fucking beer ... incredible.

"Drink the damn beer and get me one. Break open one of those kilos and give me a blast. I'm not going to hell sober," I yell.

It was gorgeous weather before we left La Hormiga in Putumayo Province this morning. There wasn't a cloud in the deep blue Colombian sky. We spent two days trekking through the jungle before this morning to purchase 60 kilos of pure uncut cocaine straight from the processing plant. We purchased the cocaine at a discounted price; buying direct from the producers cutting out a variety of middle men. The cost was $900 a kilo that will yield $24,000 a kilo in the States. The $55,000 to purchase the cocaine is money from two investors in Costa Rica, Johnny, and myself. The end result should gross somewhere around $1,350,000.00 after expenses, split between the four of us, the cut depending on the percentage of cash invested. It's just speculation providing all goes as planned. There have been a variety of costs to finance this expedition. From our plane fare, lodging, meals, and incidentals, to the lackeys to mule the cocaine out of the jungle to the plane. A plane costing us $1,500 plus tip for a one-eyed pilot and a V-

Tailed Beech Bonanza that has an upload of only 1,200 pounds. The boat and payments to sapos [snitches] to keep their mouths shut, paying others to give misinformation to authorities if asked. There's bribes and payoffs as well as other costs associated with this venture.

This depends solely on the fact we aren't killed in a plane crash or shot down by FARC (Fuerzas Armadas Revolucionarias de Columbia [Revolutionary Armed Forces of Colombia]) guerillas that we neglected to pay for safe travel. Then there's the Colombian military that hopefully hasn't been tipped off by some informant. We can't ignore the cartels being notified that we cut them out of the deal by buying directly from the source. Hopefully, we should be relatively safe if we can avoid these entities and make it out of Colombia safely. However, when we hit the ground in Panama the possibility of peril starts all over again. Johnny could give a shit about those details, instead finds reason to direct his concerns to trivial matters.

Lightning crackles and thunder booms while the engine on this propped death trap moans in desperation, fighting against the storm's persistence. Salinas is singing along with Los Tigres Del Norte crackling through a single speaker that has become raspy with age.

"Here jefe tome!" Johnny commands. He places a golf ball sized rock of cocaine in my hand and pops open a bottle of beer for me.

"Is there anything else I can get for you El Rey [King]? Maybe a cigarette or parachute," he jokes.

"You think this is hilarious, don't you? You never take anything seriously!" I respond.

"You are serious enough for both of us. Always worrying for problems that haven't happened. You make your own bad ideas in your mind. Listen, we have been carnales for a long years

25

Santiago," Johnny lectures. "Together we have been robbed, beat up, shot, stabbed, arrested, put in prison, and left with nothing, not a Peso. We survived two days in the ocean when our boat sinked. You remember? You know why the sharks no chew you up? Because you are a sour taste, bitter more than limones. Always looking at the bad side of life. You are too stubborn to die and I am not ready. Just one time think of all the fun times we have together. You have nowhere to go. So tranquilo hermano and enjoy the trip. The sun shines somewhere," he preaches.

Abruptly as in a scene from a movie, we are swallowed up in a multitude of black nimbus clouds, an abyss of darkness. The Beach Bonanza moans with a sound of despair in a final attempt to resist surrendering. With its last bit of strength, the plane bursts through the thick wall of clouds into a sky of aqua, revealing the same below. We are over the Pacific and almost out of Colombian air space. The turbulence has subsided as well as the rain and the wind. Johnny shrugs his shoulders, smiles, and begins to laugh applauding the miraculous event.

"Que Rico!" I scream.

"Then times we have more money than God. Time is our friend and we are invisible. Luck of the *I wish*," Johnny says.

"Irish. It's luck of the Irish," I correct him.

"I thought you are Italian Mexican. You are Irish also?"

"Ya, Johnny, I'm a little bit of everything."

"That's true. Some pinche grunon pendejo [fucking grumpy asshole] I think you have in you too."

Salinas announces that we still have close to an hour or so until we land at Isla del Rey [Kings Island] , a large island off the Pacific

Coast of Panama. I'm convinced that was the worst forty-five minutes I've ever experienced.

"Ok, stop with the sarcasm."

There should be a truck waiting for our arrival to unload the cache and deliver us to the boat we are taking to Mexico. It's close to two days there and better than flying because we aren't on anyone's radar. Just a fishing boat drifting about the waves searching for the next large catch.

I hand over the rock of cocaine to Salinas and he crushes it in his hand, then with one quick motion places his entire palm over his nose and inhales with the force of a Hoover vacuum. I give him the beer as well, seeing he deserved a small reward for getting us safely through a storm. I'm convinced even Dorothy would admit it was a tempest spawned in hell.

I resort back to my rule of no alcohol, drugs, or shenanigans while working. Johnny is familiar with my modus operandi and chugs his beer as a display of defiance. He gives me a relaxed salute and a thumbs up. I offer a smile wanting to voice my rebuttal to his earlier comments but don't have the enthusiasm to debate him at this moment. Best to let him believe his remarks were a valid description of my character. I've got to let him win every once in a while.

There are times when I want to terminate our relationship, end it and go it alone. Although I'd surely miss his gruffy voice along with his hysterical laugh. I'd probably worry about his welfare constantly wondering who was looking out for him. There always seems to be some type of catastrophe hovering over our heads when we participate in an operation like this as partners. Events of cataclysmic proportion materialize from somewhere beyond my ability to offer a rational explanation for their cause. It happens in most cases by no fault of our own actions.

There is one element that I'm absolutely convinced of concerning Johnny Rico, he would defend me to his death if the situation called for it. He would take a bullet for me and I would do the same. Trust is a rare commodity in this business, in this lifetime, and I trust JR. Hell, there were times in my past when I was the only friend I had and I wasn't sure he was one I could trust.

Skies clear with the sweet scent of redemption, it's fragrance replacing the smell of fear. Long thin wispy cirrus fingers scratch at the sky as though angels were keying the paint on God's celestial blue Buick.

Salinas is sweating profusely, his eyes owl sized, doing the cocaine lip smack.

"Dame otra cerveca patron!" [Give me another beer boss] Salinas demands.

Johnny immediately responds, grabbing two from the cooler and popping off the bottle caps with his teeth. I'm uncomfortable with both of them slamming beers but it was my faux pas earlier giving Salinas the coke and a beer in the first place. Johnny stares at me sporting a determined expression contemplating my reaction. He's expecting me to voice my objection to them drinking but I remain mute without expressing my concerns.

The seat at last forms comfortably around my body. An hour to relax before we reach Panama.

There's a new President that has seized power in Panama City. It's rumored he's partial to those of us that dabble in the import/export business.

The new President: Manuel Noriega.

Get Forked

"Johnny wake up man. I think you need to take me to the hospital. Come on, wake up!"

"What? What's going on Bigotes? You have asthma attack? Where is your bomba?" He sits up in bed and turns on the lamp on the nightstand.

"No Johnny, that crazy bitch stabbed me in the back. I can't tell if I'm bleeding or how deep the knife is stuck in . Whatever you do don't pull it out, I'll bleed to death before we get to the hospital."

"Okay. Okay, tranquilo carnal, let me take a look."

"Johnny, I'm serious, don't fuck around." I turn my back to him so he can get a closer look.

"Santiago, I don't think it is a knife in your back. I think maybe it is a fork she stab you with. What did you do to make her to stab you with a fork?"

"A fork? Are you sure? Take another look. Look closer. Johnny, turn on the other light." He finds the switch for the ceiling light to get a better idea of the wound's severity.

"Yes, Bigotes, it is a fork not a knife. You should have me pull it out. I don't know if it is in very deep."

"Wait, let me think about it for a minute."

"Santi, tell me why she stab you?"

"She wanted more cocaine and more cocaine and more cocaine. She was acting all strange and sketchy. I told her there wasn't anymore, she got pissed off, started screaming at me, calling me

29

a liar. I got up out of the bed, started putting on my clothes to get away from her, then I felt her stab me. She picked up her shit and ran out the door. Where'd you find that psycho-bitch man?"

"She is my cousin from Medellin."

"What the hell. Of course, another crazy person from your family. I should've figured as much. Are all your relatives mentally ill? I thought you were calling her prima [cousin] as a nickname. Like when I joke and call prostitutes 'prima'."

"I know, I am sorry. Everyone in my family is crazy with mental problems. I'm so lucky I have nothing wrong with me."

"Are you serious? You've gotta be joking. You're the craziest, Psycho-Colombiano, mentally unstable individual I've ever been associated with."

"Bigotes, why you say such mean things to me? I sometimes get crazy in a party way or when I get drunk and stuff but that's all. Maybe you can get somebody else to take the fork out. You don't want some crazy person doing it."

"Sorry Rico, I don't mean anything by it. You know I love you despite your quirks. I try to apologize. Okay, let's get the fucking fork out of my back and see what kind of damage we're dealing with here."

"There is not a lot of blood, Bigotes. But she sure pushed it deep. I didn't know a fork could be a dangerous weapon. Okay, you are ready?"

"No, I'm not ready. But go ahead and do it anyway."

"Wait, I think maybe I should have a towel in case, maybe, you start bleeding a lot. Then we need to have the cut *circlesized* with alcohol for no infection. Oh no, I hope you will not need *switches* the hospital is very far away, Bigotes."

I begin laughing from Johnny mispronouncing words and giving the incident an entirely different aspect. He's acting so dramatically I can't help but find it amusing. I don't remember when I've seen him so serious as though he is a doctor giving me a prognosis.

"Why you laughing, Bigotes? Because you don't want to cry?"

"No Johnny, I was laughing at the words you used in English. I'm very proud of you J.R. you have come a long way with learning English, but sometimes you say a word incorrectly or mispronounce a word and it ends up being humorous. I'm not making fun of you my friend, it's just funny."

"So, what you think, I'm funny? Funny like what. like a clown? I what, I make you laugh? How am I funny?"

"Now that's hilarious Johnny! You remembered that from <u>Good Fellas</u>. You do it better than Joe Pesci, very good." I'm laughing hysterically, and I start applauding his performance but it causes the fork to move around and I instantly become uncomfortable.

"I always want to do that. I'm happy you laugh. Tell me what words I say wrong when I get back with a towel and some alcohol. I think we can use tequila. Is there still some Patron left?"

"Yes, it's in the freezer. Good thinking, Johnny."

He returns drinking from the bottle of tequila. "Now we are ready, you think? Yes?"

"Let's do it!"

The fork was stuck in my left lower shoulder in the ancestis, the spot on your back that you're unable to reach to scratch. I still had my shirt on with the fork having been stuck through it. Slowly I took off the shirt so Johnny had quick access, it just hung there on the shaft.

"Bigotes, I don't know if I can do it."

"For Christ's sake J.R. Just pull the God damn fork out. Do it! It won't hurt. In fact, give me the bottle of tequila. I need a drink."

"Maybe you should drink more to not feel pain."

"Good idea again buddy. You're really showing your smarts. Ooh, you know what, I have some Vicodin in my jacket. Can you grab it for me please?"

Johnny returns with my jacket in hand sporting a huge grin. "Look what you have in the pocket. Here are the pills, look what else you're hiding, a small vial filled with cocaine and two puros that we forget to smoke at the beach. Now take your medicine and when you feel no pain, we will take out the fork."

It was 3:45 in the morning and it's not like I had to go to work or anything. Plus, I'd been wounded in action and could lounge around all day. I think it's Saturday anyway and I don't have any appointments on my calendar, so here we go. I swallowed a couple Vicodin, snorted a cap full of cocaine, then Johnny passed me the bottle of tequila. I took a long swig.

"Now let me explain why I was laughing earlier. I think you meant to say sterilize but you said *circlesize* which sounds similar to the word circumcised which has a totally different meaning. Circumcise is when a doctor cuts the extra skin off the penis of a baby boy."

"Why they do such a thing?"

"It was started by the ancient Egyptians then practiced by the Jewish people and on and on. I'm not going to get into the reasons."

"So you have *circhimsize*? I see your pene is different from mine. I am no *circhimsize* I still have the skin."

"Ya, I know Rico, I don't want to be talking about our dicks, okay?" I quickly changed the subject.

"Stitches are what the doctor sews you up with when you have a large cut. I think you said *switches*. You understand?"

Johnny lights a joint and passes it over to me. "I have a question. Why you always call marijuana *Trisumman*? Why does it have that name?"

Again, I start laughing.

"Hey, now I am going to get very angry, you laugh at me more."

"Sorry Rico, I'm saying, 'try some man' and you put all three words together. Guess I say it too fast, and it sounds like one word."

Johnny now finds the humor in what I'm saying and begins chuckling. We sat there talking and joking with Johnny doing all sorts of imitations now that I had been amused by the Joe Pesci he did. They weren't very funny but I laughed anyway. I think because I was a little drunk, Vicodin high, coked up, and stoned. Then we were startled by banging on the front door. I looked at the clock and it was 5:20 and I still had the fork in my back, although feeling no pain.

"Who the hell do you think that could be?" I whisper. "You think that bitch called the police?"

"I don't know, but I will go to the door and see. Okay? Just relax, I will take care of it."

"Thanks Johnny."

He staggers to the front door, and I take cover around the corner of the front room within hearing distance.

"Quien es acá?" [Who's here?] Johnny asks.

I don't understand why he just doesn't look out the window on the side. I hear a woman's voice but not well enough to know what she's saying.

"Esperame uno segundo." [Wait a second.] I hear him answer. He walks back in the bedroom shaking his head and chuckling.

"Bigotes, it is my cousin again. She has no money for taxi or bus and wants to say she is sorry to you."

"What do you think? Does she seem normal to you, not all weird?"

"I'm not sure. You make the call."

"Okay let her in but don't let her come near me."

He goes to the door swinging it open but stepping back out the way. She struts in and walks straight toward me.

"Hey Rico, you better get over here."

"Don't worry Santiago, I'm not going to do anything to you. I want to say I'm sorry and to make it up to you. I didn't hurt you real bad, did I?"

"You stabbed me in the back with a fucking fork! Here, take a look." I turn my back to her, so she can see her handy work. Then

34

I feel her hand grab the fork and with a swift motion she pulls it out.

"I'm so sorry baby, let me make it up to you."

She drops her dress on the living room floor, grabs my hand leading me into my bedroom.

"So, you have some more cocaine?" She purrs.

Mickey Sixpence

Johnny and I had just gotten out of the Carlos Vivas concert along with our dates for the evening. I suggested we head to one of my favorite restaurants for a late-night meal. Everyone was in agreement since I offered to buy. Slowly, rhythmically, like a Mozart second movement, arm in arm, I walked with my incredibly attractive date. We were strolling behind Johnny and his girl and of course he had his hand on her ass. We had just gotten back after successfully finishing a "run" from Mexico to Los Angeles. A celebration was warranted to lose the jitters we both still suffered from the close call we had encountered during this smuggling event.

It was a short distance to the Lincoln Town Car I'd recently purchased from a misfortunate pendejo [idiot]. He was busted and given an eight-year; all expenses paid vacation for robbing a high-end jewelry store. In an attempt to fence the cache quickly, he unknowingly dealt with the cousin of the owner whose store he had robbed. It is a nice enough ride, but sometimes it becomes difficult to maneuver on some of the city's narrow streets and tight turns. It was still a righteous purchase, and his wife appreciated the cash especially with three children to raise on her own.

So along with the Mighty Big Car, I toyed with the idea to hire a chauffeur. The opportunity to find someone presented itself. I couldn't turn down this colorful character's request for employment.

"Pleased to meet you mate, they call me Mickey Sixpence. I'm originally from New Castle, on the Tyne, United Kingdom," is how he introduced himself. He mentioned that he doesn't like New Castle Ale and the New Castle United Fútbol Team are a bunch of wankers. Then in a polite tone he requested I don't refer to those subjects if I attempt to make small talk.

We met at the casino one night and he had lost all of his money. He asked me if there might be a chance I could float him a few quid until his pension was deposited. Now I had no fucking idea how much a few quid was but I told him I'd lend him fifty dollars but first I would need to know who he was and where he lived and worked. His apartment, it turned out, was across the street from mine. He wasn't employed at the time, but worked as a chauffeur back in the U.K. for some very distinguished and infamous clients.

I found him to be a nice enough guy. As I started to hand him the money, he began giving me his pitch on why I should hire him.

"You know something? I am sure you could use my services. I see you every once in a while, driving that big Lincoln of yours and I think you'd enjoy being chauffeured around. I know this city like it was my hometown, and we can negotiate my salary. I can make myself available twenty-four seven. Also, I'm one hell of a bodyguard as well. And I keep my mouth shut. How do you feel about that, Boss?"

"The name is Santiago, don't call me Boss. Give me a day to think about it and I'll let you know."

"Fair enough, Boss."

I hired him without questioning his character, something I seldom do. He's turned out to be a decent and entertaining employee. Johnny appreciates having him around; they get along famously with one another and communicate on the same low frequency.

Mickey is a large fellow with enormous fists missing some knuckles. It's obvious he's been in his fair share of street scuffles. His head is shaved, you can tell his nose has been broken a few times, much like mine. He has a boisterous laugh , complemented with a scary kind of smile. I guess he's maybe thirty-five years old, and drinks his gin and tonic without the lime. Something about not wanting people to call him 'Limey' along with some bullshit about having had a couple of distant relatives killed while fighting during the Crusades. He pointed out all they accomplished was bringing back the lime and introducing it to the U.K. I thought it made for an interesting subplot and called on him to tell the story on a few occasions. The one fact I found somewhat bizarre, as well as humorous, was his desire to become a professional ventriloquist with an astounding act he already had worked out and is sure audiences will clamor for.

Everybody has to have a dream, an aspiration, a goal in life, the desire to be somebody. He talks with a robust Georgie English accent that when he speaks Spanish it has the inflection of a distinct juxtaposition. It could be best described as listening to Classical music in a biker bar.

We turned a corner into a street which was dark with just a few working streetlights. I instantly became cautious, and I wanted Johnny to be aware of my suspicion.

"Hey carnal." I softly said to get J.R.'s attention.

"Yo sé jefe. Soy listo [I know chief. I'm ready]," he answered back.

The Town Car came into view as we walked past a hardware store with delivery trucks parked out front.

Then like a Chicago Saturday night, gunshots rang out from an automatic rifle with bullets penetrating the delivery trucks with some pinging off of the brick building. I assumed it was an AK-47 because they're a very popular choice of gang members here.

Without delay we took cover behind a dump truck. I returned fire with my Glock toward a dumpster where I had noticed some rifle flashes. Johnny crouched down next to me with the girls safely hiding in the store's brick entryway. I fired off a couple more rounds, then Johnny followed suit firing two shots from his antique .38 Police Special.

"I'm out." Johnny reports.

"What do ya mean you're out?"

"I'm out. You know, I don't have any more bullets. I'm out."

"You only fired twice. You're telling me you only had two bullets loaded in your pistol? Well reload dumbshit. What are you waiting for?" I ordered.

I could see the answer in his eyes before he said a word.

"So that's all you brought with you is two rounds? What if we got into a shootout and needed to defend ourselves? Wait a second, call me Nostradamus, that's exactly what's happening right now!"

"Don't holler at me Santi, I will not ever let it happen again. I'm sorry."

"Let me see if I can talk to these guy's and find out why they're shooting at us. Maybe I can negotiate a ceasefire."

I hollered out into the darkness hoping to open a line of communication. "Hey, what is the problem here? Who are you guys and why are you shooting at us?"

"Because you are going with my girlfriend Carmen, and I am very mad by it." A voice from the darkness responds.

"That's Carmen's crazy ass boyfriend, Rodrigo. He is a jealous pendejo and she has not been with him for a long time," my date Diana yells.

"It is true. Rodrigo follows me all the time and makes trouble for me," Carmen, Johnny's date says.

"So did you know about this telenovela [soap opera] drama story before you decided to ask her out?" I interrogate Johnny.

"She said ..." he stops explaining.

"What is going on?" The psycho ex-boyfriend screams.

"Hold on Rodrigo, give us a minute we're working this out," I yell out hoping to buy us some time.

"This guy is going through a lot of trouble to win her back. All he has to do is kill her cat and hang it in front of her door. Right Johnny?"

"You are now not a very funny guy. Why are you laughing?"

"You know why I'm laughing? Out of all the women in this city you choose this woman with a psycho boyfriend stalking her. What's wrong with you Rico?" Johnny doesn't answer. He hangs his head down, mumbling to himself. "Carmen, what do you want to do?" I ask the psycho's ex-girlfriend.

"Carmen, come here talk to me." Rodrigo pleads.

"No, Rodrigo, go away I don't want to be with you anymore."

With that, a burst of automatic gunfire rings out. It wasn't the response I was hoping for.

"So, Johnny, I have no role in this lover's spat. I'm going to get my date and go. You can deal with the jealous psychopath yourself. This is all your doing."

"Santiago, are you being a joker? Please don't leave me alone. This pendejo is a crazy one. I think he might kill me."

"Carmen, come here now," Rodrigo yells.

Suddenly some headlights come up behind us and the car squeals to a stop sitting sideways toward the action. Mickey exits the Lincoln with an automatic rifle laying down a line of defensive fire. "Come on, hurry, get in, Boss," Mickey commands while once again firing off more rounds.

I ran over to Diana, grabbed her hand, pulled her out and into the Lincoln. I don't have any idea how, but Johnny and Carmen were both already inside. Closing the door, I tell Mickey we're ready. He fires off another burst, hops into the car, puts it in gear and with tires screeching and smoking we are gone.

"Good form, Mickey. Where in the hell did you get the automatic rifle?" I ask.

"I always keep one in the trunk. Spare tire, jack, and automatic rifle. I'm always prepared. Told you I was a damn good bodyguard." Mickey says over his shoulder with a laugh.

"I never said I doubted you. Once again thanks carnal."

"No problem, just doing my job Boss. Where to?"

Los Dos Chiflados
[The Two Whacky Guys]

The picture tube has gone out on the television, but the sound still works scratching through worn out brittle speakers. A male voice in Spanish is explaining the necessary ingredients required to make Christmas Tamales. They are a traditional treat served in every home in Colombia during the holidays. He tells the audience he's going to divulge a secret recipe that has been in his family since Simon Bolivar was President of Colombia (1819-1830). The audience responds with "oohs" and "aahs" expressing their astonishment at the news.

These aren't anything similar to the typical Mexican Tamales served in Chicano restaurants in the United States. Colombian Bogotano Tamales, one of three popular types made in Colombia, are unique. They are much larger than Mexican Tamales. These are stuffed full of generous portions of pork and chicken. Potatoes, carrots, chickpeas, and a pepper are also added. They are packed together in a spiced masa that is wrapped in a banana leaf and tied with string to hold it together while they are steamed for an hour and a half or so on a low heat. They're a culinary delight everyone should sample once in their lifetime. Surprisingly, Johnny Rico makes some of the best Bogotano Tamales I've ever tasted. Although I was stoned every time I ate them.

Christmas is just a week away and Johnny is two days late with the cocaine he's driving from Cali to here in Cartagena. We're supposed to deliver the load by the twenty-fourth to its final destination in Louisiana.

I'm feeling somewhat guilty that I didn't accompany him on the trip. I had a problem with immigration concerning my visa being expired. It was a serious issue I needed to address immediately. The wheels of government agencies don't always move swiftly in

Colombia and it could take two to three days to correct depending on the attitude of the official in charge. Fortunately, it took only a day to correct and I was issued a new ninety day visa. I attribute the quick fix to the immigration official being under the influence of the Holiday Spirit.

I could've sent Mickey Sixpence with him if he had still been around. However, his employment was short-lived along with my ownership of the Lincoln Town Car. Without my knowledge, Mickey had been moonlighting and using the Lincoln as well. He was found murdered in the car with twenty-nine gunshots to his body. Strange, but I wondered how many bullet holes had penetrated my car. I had developed strong emotional ties to it and was more saddened by the loss of the Lincoln than Mickey after finding out about his betrayal.

There were fifty kilos of cocaine found in the car along with Mickey's body. He had been working for a cartel, doing short runs from city to city. It was a rival cartel and we weren't associated with it in any way. Later, I received an apology from my Jefe for not informing me prior to the execution of the execution. The car had never been registered in my name, so I had no connection to the murder or the drugs.

This wasn't typical Johnny behavior. He may at times not think through a situation before reacting but he has never been so late before or not called and reported his status. Of course, me being the "Master of Doom and Gloom," I've imagined the worst scenario possible with every passing hour.

This was to be our third "run" for this Patron [Boss] out of Putumayo. The other two times we completed the smuggling operation without complication. He was impressed and so delighted with our past performances; he even gave us a bonus. After completing this Donkey-Haul we were planning on asking El Patron permission to work independently as outside contractors in business for ourselves. Although we weren't exactly active members of the cartel, the other cartels considered us soldiers. If there was a feud or vendetta with some other cartel or gang we'd be considered the enemy and be dealt with accordingly. There'd be no time for explanations. Being independent would give us dispensation, plus we would then be welcomed in Mexico. I'm not sure if you're aware of the fact that Mexicans and Colombians aren't very fond of each other.

We were familiar with all the contacts in Mexico, Panama, El Salvador, and Colombia and we had a stellar and untarnished reputation. However, we would be discouraged from dealing with any of their clientele. It was fine with us, we had buyers lined up in Tucson, Phoenix, Austin, San Diego, and Chicago.

We had gained the reputation as reliable and trustworthy 'runners'. There were those who questioned our sanity due to the methods we've used to complete our missions. We are referred to by most Jefes [Chiefs] as "Los dos Chiflados". Roughly translated it means, 'The Two Whacky Guys'. Johnny is nicknamed 'Tornillo Zafado" which means 'loose screw'. He really despises the nickname but laughs whenever a cartel member calls him by the name. I don't think he realizes his reaction causes fear in most of them. His lunatic laugh lends proof of his insanity.

I guess the possibility of us becoming self-employed is teetering on the abyss. Of course, why would it be any different? This is the way fate has determined it shall forever be and my destiny is always having to rise to the challenge.

I turn down the sound on the television as I walk to the window but don't turn it off thinking the picture may be resurrected. The entire avenue can be viewed from my second story window. The rain has finally halted and the street below that was completely vacant a few minutes ago is quickly filled with street pharmacists, addicts, and prostitutes. It's not your typical *Christmas Story* scene but this is my life, the one I've created for myself. Here I am starring in my own Dickens-like movie.

It's so damn hot and I'm sweating like a defendant waiting for the jury to announce the verdict. This summer has been brutal with rain causing extreme humidity because of high temperatures. The only sound in my apartment is the fan's metal blades rattling lies about producing a breeze. Once again there's no water, which occurs daily and I use water saved for cooking and drinking to wash away the sweat from my face.

It's just a couple minutes past 11:00 pm on a Saturday night in Cartagena and the sound of gunfire has started early. I don't usually venture out alone at night. I'm fairly well known by most of the derelicts, gang members, and thieves. That's not the issue. My fear is being caught in the middle of a gunfight and getting shot by a stray bullet. It's a common event in my neighborhood.

I change the channel on the T.V. to the one with music videos. Brushing away the cockroaches on the sofa and slapping the cushions is a temporary solution to get rid of them. I lie on my plush sofa closing my eyes listening to Carlos Vivas. Once again, the rain starts coming down with a punishing force. The pinging of raindrops on the metal roof is in perfect tempo with the song. However, the rain is coming in through the windows but it's too hot to close them, praying for the hint of a breeze.

There's a knock at my door that startles me awake. I didn't know I had fallen asleep or for how long. The rain has taken a break and the breeze dances through the room. Again, a knock.

"Santiago, are you there? It's Johnny, open the door pinche!" My friend hollers.

"Voy carnal," I responded. I get up to answer the door, but slip on the wet tile floor from the rain. My body slams down to the floor and I hear a muffled crack from my left arm followed by excruciating pain.

"Goddamn it! Hold on for a minute Johnny, I slipped and fell on the wet floor, and I think my arm is broken." I cry out.

"Come on, don't screw around. I'm not in the mood for your jokes."

I try to get up but the pain from moving my arm is too much to bear. "Johnny, use the key hidden outside under the fire extinguisher. I can't get up right now. I'm sure I broke my arm."

"Okay, I'll be right back."

My arm is beginning to swell and is already black and blue. Finally, I make it to my feet and sit down on the couch holding my arm still with my right hand.

"I can't find no key on under fire *stinger*."

"Try opening the door. Maybe it's not even locked," I suggest. I watch the knob turn and then a click. It swings open revealing my buddy standing outside the door with his arm in a sling, his head wrapped in gauze and both eyes black and blue. "Did you even think of trying to open the door to see if it was locked?" I holler despite my pain.

"Tell me is the load okay? What in the hell happened to you, Rico? Did you finally get caught in bed with some guy's wife? He sure did a job on you." I laugh.

"You see me like this and all you do is make jokes? Then you ask about the load, not how I am. The load is safe. How is your arm? It doesn't look so good. It is all blacked with blue. Do you think it's broked?"

"I'm sure it is. Let me put my shoes on and we'll grab a taxi to the hospital. Be careful walking, the floor is all wet from the rain, you know how slick they can get. You can tell me what happened to you on the way there and why you didn't call. Good to see you, Johnny. I was worried about you and concerned that no one would be able to contact me and I'd miss your funeral."

"Why do you say things like that and give the spirits ideas to use against us? You know I'm super *switches* and don't like it when you say things like that."

"You mean superstitious?" I tell him while walking down the stairs to grab a taxi. "I'm sorry, Johnny, but I don't understand your religious dogma or even what religion you follow. It's like you just make up commandments." I tell him as we get into the taxi.

The hospital is a twenty-minute drive which should give Johnny plenty of time to make up a lie to explain his tardiness, if he hasn't already concocted a story.

"Why you bring up dogs to my religion Santiago? I like dogs very much but don't think they are spirits to me."

"No, no, no. Dogma means the principles a religion follows. It has nothing to do with dogs. Sorry I wasn't poking fun at you," I apologize.

"Now tell me what in the hell happened to you? The load is okay, you're sure?"

"Yes, the load is okay. When I passed Bogota late at night the mountain road was very twisted. I pulled to the side of the road to park because I had to go pee real bad. It was very dark and when I step to the side of the road it all fell down along with me. I tried to climb up but there was no way. I banged my head on big rocks and was bleeding also I have arm fracture. My phone got lost and don't have your number in my memory. I waited for a car to pass then I would yell out. For almost two days I was down there and no one comes to help. Finally, a farmer stopped to check on the problem with the truck and he hear me holler then help me out. He have his son drive my truck to follow to the hospital. So, I drive here after eight hours in hospital. I think I was going to die down there, Santiago."

"That story is too good for you to make up, it's gotta be true. I'm glad you are okay. I was truly worried about you carnal. So, do you still want to do this job? I can call El Jefe and explain our situation. Maybe he'll give us a few days to recover. That way we can celebrate Christmas together. You make your famous tamales and you can buy me presents. Then after we deliver the load we'll spend the new year in New Orleans. How does that sound to you?"

"First let's see about your arm and I want to tell you now that you have blood coming from the back of your head, maybe you need ..."

"Stitches?"

"Yes, those things. I have six in my head. I need to get them out in five days. I also have fracture in my arm but doctor put on cast to make it heal faster."

"You sure have been through hell. Okay, we've got some options to consider. Let's discuss it when we get back to the apartment. I've gotta check with Demonio Mosca to see if he can fly us later than planned. Then I'll call El Jefe and check out the possibility of a short delay."

We reached the hospital and the taxi driver tried to overcharge us by twenty-five dollars. He heard us speaking English and thought we were easy marks. Immediately, Johnny begins yelling insults and profanities at the taxi driver telling him now that we aren't paying anything. He starts reading off the driver's name license number and taxi plate number from his license displayed on the dashboard.

"My mother is a Commissioner at the Ministry of Transportation. I'll make sure she is told about your dishonest practice," Johnny tells the now apologetic driver.

He begs Johnny not to report him, he might lose his license and has five hungry mouths to feed. He says there's no charge for the taxi ride. Johnny accepts his offer promising not to report him to the ministry.

"Well, that was quite a trick. Where did you pick up that con?"

"From you. You do it one time in Mexico City."

We both laugh on cue while walking into the Emergency Room entrance but stop immediately as we enter inside. Of course, it is packed with at least seventy-five people all waiting to be seen by one of the two doctors available.

Johnny drags me to the triage desk that is vacant without anyone available. A nurse appears and Johnny begins to explain my injuries. After listening to his explanation, she tells him she works in admitting and we'll have to wait for a triage nurse.

"Santiago, fall down on the floor now." Johnny whispers.

"Do I pretend to pass out or do I pretend I'm dead?"

He gives me a disgusted glare while pushing me down. Just before hitting the floor, he catches my body saving me from making contact. Although he grabs my left arm and I let out a horrific terrifying scream. It causes a pain that rushes through my entire body.

"Good Santi. That is very good. You sound like you have pain," Johnny whispers again.

"I do have pain, you're squeezing my broken arm pendejo. Let go!" I say softly.

He releases his grip and my arm flops to the floor and I respond with a scream that echoes throughout the hospital. It definitely gets the attention of some hospital staff.

"Is that a real scream?" He asks.

"Please, somebody help my cousin. He is hurt bad," he pleads in Spanish.

A doctor, a couple interns and a few nurses come running to assist me. They ask Johnny what happened and what type of injuries I may have sustained. Now he could've just said I slipped on a wet tile floor. It's a common occurrence causing all types of injuries. Not Johnny, he has to create a horrifying incident that will capture the interest of the hospital staff. No boring common slip and fall story.

"There was a big riot fight by gangs on Calle Rio Blanco. We try to run away and hide but some guys catch Santiago and start beating him with metal poles, kicking at him, too. I run back to him and start hitting the punks with a metal pole I found. I hit them with some bricks I threw at them and they ran away."

"You're a hero, and probably saved your cousin's life," a cutie nurse comments placing her hand on Johnny's back.

"But what happened to you? Are you okay? Where did you get your injuries?" The cutie nurse inquires.

"I got these on my way here from Bogota from FARC Guerillas. They rob me and beat me up."

"Well, you've had quite an action packed past two days. We're going to take your cousin to X-ray and let us take a look at you as

50

well. Just to make sure you are okay," Doctor Bad Breath says. They load me onto a gurney and the doctor begins examining me walking alongside as they roll me to X-ray.

"Come with me to an examination room and we'll wait for the doctor to take a look at you," I hear the pretty nurse tell Johnny while leading him away, holding his hand and rubbing his shoulder. I look back at him and he flashes a Cheshire Cat grin.

Johnny Rico, my hero!

Do You Ever Think About Me

It had been years since we last saw one another. I felt somewhat uncomfortable by this chance meeting. I didn't remember if we parted on good terms. I knew the majority of my relationships ended with profanities being screamed at me, various cooking utensils were thrown with the intention of causing severe bodily injury, the occasional death threats and I was shot at more times than I care to mention. Odds are our breakup wasn't at all cordial. The conversation seemed awkward with both of us searching for something to say during a couple of instances of uncomfortable silence.

"What if, I might ask, are you doing back in New Orleans? You don't live here, do you?" She asked.

"No, just visiting. I've got some business to attend to that'll take a few days. Then, I'll be heading to Tucson to see my children."

"You still refer to your illegal transportation of contraband a business. You must think I'm stupid or suffer from brain damage."

"I never told you my work is illegal. I'd prefer not to discuss the subject any longer."

"Fair enough. Are you still hanging around with that degenerate friend, Johnny Rico?"

"As a matter of fact, he's getting a haircut right now. I'm waiting for him to be done. And you know, Johnny has never had a bad word to say about you. Whenever he made a comment referring to your character, he always expressed your personality in a favorable light."

"You're absolutely correct. I was demonstrating displaced aggression when you're the one I'm upset with. I didn't intend to act like a bitch."

"It's forgotten. You can't help being you."

"That was not the correct response to my comment if you intend to get back on my good side," explaining herself without actually accepting blame.

"So which side is your good side? I can't figure it out."

"Listen up, smart ass, you're pushing the envelope. Better watch your words."

There was a question I wanted to ask but I knew it wouldn't be a good idea. It just wasn't the right time, especially after sabotaging our chance encounter. So, of course, I went ahead and asked anyway.

"Do you ever think about me?"

"Yes, I do," she quickly answered. "More than I'd care to admit."

I smiled, feeling somewhat flattered.

"Although, you should know that when I do think of you the thoughts aren't complimentary. I just don't have any good memories of our time together."

"What do you mean? I remember wonderful times when we lived together in ... ahh."

"What's wrong? You've got me mixed up with one of your floozies. We lived together here in New Orleans, genius. Then you took off to Costa Rica and abandoned me without ever contacting me again. Does that sound at all familiar to you? Do you even remember my name? Tell me, what is it?" Expressing her disdain.

"I don't know what I was thinking. My memory has been experiencing a glitch lately. Of course, I remember your name. What do you take me for? You never gave me a chance to explain. When I got back you had moved. Your number was disconnected and the people you worked with at the Herb Shoppe wouldn't give me any information."

"That's possibly true. They knew how hurt I was by the way you treated me."

"I didn't intend to hurt you in any way. I apologize if I caused you emotional pain, Simone."

"So, you do remember my name? And now you can forget it because there will never be a need to say it again." Then with a confident expression she turned, walked away, and never looked back, without even saying 'Goodbye.'

I walked the short distance to the barbershop where I noticed Johnny standing outside carrying on a conversation with three New Orleans cops. I could hear the distinct sound of Johnny's laughter along with the cops adding to the chorus of merriment. Johnny introduced me to the three female Crescent City law officers. We talked for five minutes or so and bid the ladies good fortune and farewell. I hollered out my TV show quote, "Y'all be careful out there." They smiled, then waved, disappearing around the corner.

"Hey, you'll never guess who I bumped into at Audubon Park."

"That witch you live with here, with a man's name. 'Simon' I think and she stick doll with pins making voodoo on you. I am right?"

"Ya Simone, you're right, sometimes you really amaze me. It didn't go well. She always had a tendency to be derogatory and condescending."

"If those words mean act like a bitch, then now you are right. How many times I tell you she is a bitch but worse than that she was a bruja, witch. But she is a very pretty witch."

Well, so I guess you figured out that I was less than truthful when telling Simone Johnny has never spoken a derogatory word about her. I'm a little concerned about how she will feel about our meeting. I certainly hope not to experience any sharp stabbing pains like I felt after our initial breakup. Maybe I should have been more courteous. Screw it, I don't believe in witchcraft.

Ouch!

Psychopath Merit Badge

I could see the angels dancing in his eyes before I blew out his fucking brains. The pistol was pressed firmly against his left temple, sunlight glimmering off the chrome barrel. Although somewhat off key, the Fat Lady was singing and not some Reggae song. It was over for this "sapo," the fucking snitch. This Rasta Rat Bastard on his knees in front of me was at the mercy of my omnipotent finger pressed against the trigger. He cost me three years of my life, spent in hell's waiting room, a filthy shithole prison in Bogota, Colombia. Now my name was "Karma" and death was on the menu. His tongue refrained from requesting mercy, he knew there were no words to detour his fate. A small thunder crackled as the bullet exited the muzzle piercing his skull. It rattled around inside his cranium spitting out his brain's red ink spelling the obvious message.

I invested seven months tracking down this Son of a Bitch that sold me out to Federal Police to save his own ass from incarceration. You always rat up, ya never rat down, and evidently, I was a necessary ingredient in the authorities recipe for justice soup. They busted my ass thirty minutes after the boat, ladened with two hundred and fifty kilos of cocaine was six kilometers from shore. We were heading to Nicaragua and after making landfall, points beyond. It was to be my windfall run, my magnum opus of the drug smuggling trade. All the time spent planning, the money that two partners and I had personally invested, as well as the bribes and payoffs that were disbursed, had all been wasted. The vision of a wealthy epilogue to the undertaking disintegrated into seconds of my life ticking away in jail. I felt no remorse by my act of vengeance, nor did I feel I was malevolent or sinister by whacking the Jamaican piece of shit wrapped in skin. I actually did him a favor by not employing the Colombian cartel brand of street justice. I let his wife and children live.

I left his crumpled body laying in the jungle's elephant grass on top of a pile of banana tree leaves whose silvery backside were now spotted with Jackson Pollock like splotches of red. It was already starting to draw flies and mosquitos. The process of decay in the jungle is a quick and effective manner of environmentally friendly recycling.

"That's cold blooded, Bigotes. I have never seen that demon inside of you before. I hope to never have you mad at me. Never!" Johnny Rico spoke from behind me as we trudged through the underbrush up the hill to the road.

"Here Rico, take the gun." I said while passing it back to him without stopping.

"Gracias, I feel safer now carnal. The pistol has blood and tiny pieces of his brain all over it man!" Johnny moaned.

"Get rid of the piece, Rico! No mistakes. Ya hear me? Entiendas?" I yelled.

"Ok Carnal, but you already make one big mistake," he answered back.

"Ya, you think so? What was that? What are you saying, Rico?"

"You didn't kill him twice. Now you are fucked. His spirit will haunt you and visit your dreams. Always kill something twice. You never listen to me. You will never learn," he preached.

"Stop with that Caribbean voodoo , black magic, Juju bullshit. I don't believe in God and certainly lend no credence to that crap! Shut the fuck up, Johnny! I've a lot on my mind, give me a break," I ordered.

"Ok Bigotes, but I too like that band very much forever. Run through the jungle. Run through the jungle. Good song for now, I think Jefe, Creedence," he sings.

Sometimes it's just better to let his incorrect references go unedited than try to explain what I meant by credence. It'll save me two hours of frustration. My sweat begins to mix with the blood that has splattered on my hands and arms forming pink droplets staining my white shorts and also my shoes. Suddenly, a feeling of extreme despair runs through my body like a current of electricity. I realize that there is only one thing separating me from a psychopath and that is the feeling of remorse for what I had done. Even all the years of Catholicism that had been beaten into me by ruler wielding nuns couldn't compel me to produce a single tear or an emotion of shame or guilt. So, I've earned my 'Psychopath Merit Badge.'

I felt righteously justified in killing the informant and was looking forward to the other motherfucking "sapo" meeting with the same fate. Last information I had on his where 'bouts was Nicaragua. We had absolutely no friends there and few connections. President Ortega ran a strict Unitary Government that basically made-up laws and restrictions as situations developed. I was going to have to call in a "favor" if we were to achieve any type of success in Managua.

We reach the SUV and Johnny hops in the driver's seat and takes command of the vehicle.

"Turn off the air conditioning, Rico. I don't want to catch a cold," I ask.

"Yes, I am sure you are cold enough already. Off it goes," he jokes.

The sun was beginning to paste late afternoon shadows on the mountainsides announcing its impending departure to the world's otherside. I laid in the backseat watching the tops of palm trees flash by and one puffy gray cloud following as we head back to the hotel in Quepos.

I feel the SUV lurch to a stop and then hear a splash. Johnny has just thrown the gun into the estuary from the bridge near Dominical.

"¿Hey pinche, back to the hotel si o si?" Johnny barks.

"Si Hermano a el hotel. ¿Hey Rico?"

"¿Qué quieres [what do you want] Bigotes?"

"Tu sabes. Tu sabes [you know]," I say.

"I know, I love you too carnal," he answers.

"Hey, Bigotes, we should go out tonight. I will let you buy me dinner, then we can get some womens and get drunk like a hundred indians. How you thinking about that carnal? You need some crazy fun like in the old days when you got wild and act of a maniac. We use to have fun and be happy," Johnny says.

"Tienes razon [you're right]. A night we won't remember. But no fucking tequila for you Rico and you promise to keep your clothes on. No strip tease shows or painting your cock and displaying it as an Obra de Arte [work of art]. ¿Si o si?" I preach.

"Claro, Bigotes, but you must to do Mick Jagger Stones singer imitation and Michael Jackson dance. Those things make me laugh crazy." he says.

It would prove to be an appropriate therapy to subdue what was beginning to manifest into an obsession.

Who Doesn't Like Strawberries

"What do you mean I don't have any future left; I've used it up? How is that even possible?" I questioned.

I had no clue as to what she was talking about. It was a challenge to just listen to her rant with the monster hangover I was nursing. Now I had to make sense of what the hell she meant by her statement. Please just shoot me my dear and put me out of your misery.

"You've spent it, you're overdrawn. Similar to a cat using all nine lives, only it's your destiny I'm referring to. It's been wasted, squandered, and mismanaged. Kismet has given up, thrown in the towel. Get it smart guy?" She motions pointing to her head while making the goofy face of an idiot. "Besides your checkered past clashes with my pastel-colored future, so this relationship or whatever it is, has reached its end."

"So, help me to understand what you're saying. The fate of my future was that I would run out of destiny. I am without any tommorows because I used them up in my yesterdays? Fate is determined at birth. My destiny, however, is determined by my actions; it can't be possible. Sounds like bullshit to me!" I motion with my finger pointing to my ass. "Have you joined the Church of Scientology again? Is this your Thetan talking? You're sounding a lot like my mother, only she'd mix in some Jesus shit and top it off with some mystic witchy stuff. What is happening here, I'm completely confused?"

Why is it when relationships end it always deteriorates into name calling with intention to cause emotional scars? I would much rather walk away knowing the time we spent together was a wonderful ride that just ran out of road. This screaming and assigning blame is vindictive.

"And there it is, Mister Negative putting down a religion he knows nothing about."

"Hey, I've done my research and have developed an opinion based on deductive reasoning. Did you know L. Ron Hubbard was a science fiction author before establishing the Church of Scientology? Gives you an idea of how he came up with the doctrine for the religion. You sincerely believe you are an extraterrestrial being? You want to know what really bothers me, is who goes around calling themself L.Ron Hubbard? I find it extremely pretentious using an initial for your first name. Why? Doesn't he like the name the L represents? Are we supposed to guess the name? Does he think it adds an air of mystery about him? It's like e.e. cummings or T.S. Eliot, what the fuck is that all about. Why is it that if I'm not in favor of or advocate a movement or dislike something it means I'm negative? You didn't like *The Boys and Girls Guide to Getting Down* which is on my favorite movies list and I didn't give you any shit about your opinion. You don't like strawberries, do I accuse you of being a negative person because of your dislike of strawberries? No, I never said anything. Now that I think about it, it should've been a clue to your negative demeanor. Who doesn't like strawberries?"

"How the hell did we get to talking about this shit? I'll admit Santiago, you do have a talent for twisting a conversation into some obscure subject. I can't do this anymore. You should have seen this coming."

"How could I have seen it coming? I can't determine my future if there isn't any. Let's not do this. If you are no longer enamored with me please just say so and leave it at that. There's no need for this destructive rhetoric, it's not a healthy or worthwhile practice. Also, this isn't my first breakup, so I'm sort of an expert. I've become immune to the derogatory dialogue and insults."

"I'm more than sure of that. You're a professional when it comes to this. Of course, you've built up an immunity after all the relationships you've sabotaged."

There's no winner in these types of frays. I'm truly sorry she has built up such loathing for me. However, I'm completely without any clue as to what the hell happened here. It seemed to me we were enjoying each other's company just yesterday. Maybe she's on her ... no I'm not going to say it. Really? Y'all want me to mention it during this argument? I'm at times a bit dense when dealing with women, but I have learned there's never a right time to ask the wrong question or to answer truthfully when asked your opinion, especially concerning her appearance. All women want you to lie, it's the one of the many unwritten laws of relationship survival. And all of you want to see me persecuted. You heartless bastards. You'll have to wait for your sick entertainment at my expense in some other story.

"I'm still without a clue as to your sudden decision to break-up. I do want you to know I cherish you. You are the complete package and the man that wins your heart is truly fortunate."

"Stop with the sweet talk. I've practiced this dissertation for quite awhile. My mind is made up."

'Well, that's disheartening to hear. How long have you been practicing?"

"I'm sorry Santiago, I don't mean to act like such a bitch. I feel so ... I don't know, I'm sorry if I hurt you."

"I'm more disappointed than hurt. I need to know the reason. Let's not make this any more unpleasant than it already has become. I think it's better we don't continue with spilling any more bad blood."

"I've got one question. I would appreciate you answering honestly. I found your passport in your blazer before I took it to the drycleaners, and I looked inside. You have been everywhere in Central and South America as well as Mexico numerous times in the past three years. Then I found a second passport from Canada with a different name, your picture and the same destinations. What's up with you? What kind of work do you do? You disappear for days with no communication, then appear back without an explanation. You always speak Spanish when you're on the phone. And that friend of yours, that Donny Rico guy, there's something seriously wrong with him. He is definitely mentally ill, no joke. Have you ever looked into his eyes? They are so empty without a spark of life in them. He's definitely an alcoholic and a drug addict. What do you see in him?"

"It's Johnny, not Donny."

"What? You lied about his name?"

"No, you misinterpreted his name. Johnny is my friend, my only friend, and would never hurt anyone I was associated with. I never made condescending comments about your psycho bitch friends. Talk about basket cases, they're the most judgmental, self-righteous, backstabbing, delusional, and evil women I've ever encountered. Johnny has always been polite and courteous to you as well as respectful, isn't that true?"

She nods her head yes.

"Your friends treat me like a leper. What am I doing? I'm beginning to get defensive."

"So, what's up with you? What do you do for work? Are you going to tell me or not?"

"Why is it of any concern to you now? Since we are no longer together I don't feel I owe you any explanation. And I'm feeling a bit violated that you invaded my privacy."

"Why is it such a big secret? What, are you a spy? A secret agent like James Bond? Santiago please, just because I'm pretty doesn't mean I'm stupid." She opens a drawer in the desk then hands me the two passports. "Do you want to know what I think?"

"No, not at all. I'm not interested. In fact, I should begin packing up and find a place to stay."

"You don't have to leave immediately, tomorrow morning will be fine. I'm not going to kick you out until you've found a place." She sits down next to me on the sofa and grabs my hands.

"I asked my cousin Rodney, he is an officer with the Border Patrol, he said most likely someone with that type of background with multiple passports is probably a drug dealer or someone smuggling contraband of some kind."

"You asked who, what about me? Are you fucking insane? Your cousin is a Federal Officer? You didn't! You can't be serious."

"He's not like a real cop or anything like that, he's Border Patrol."

"Well tell all the guys doing time for drug busts that the Border Patrol aren't real cops."

"I didn't mention your name or give him any information that would implicate you. Listen, I know you're a drug dealer. Not the kind that sells to people out in the streets. No, you're one of those movie-type characters dealing in the big stuff. There's a name for them but I can't think of it right now."

"What like a, "Narco Traficante"? I blurt out.

What the fuck is wrong with me? I leave my passports in my jacket for her to find and now I identify myself as a drug trafficker. Damn, I'm a real tough nut to crack, and to top it off, I'm in a relationship with a woman who has a Federal Police Officer in the family.

"Yes! Yes, that's it, Narcotics guy. Well, are you? Tell me I promise not to tell anyone. Please. It's hard to believe because I've rarely seen you do drugs and you never seem to have much money. Tell me!"

I wasn't about to disclose any more information than I already had. For some unknown reason I couldn't come up with an embellishment to explain my vocation.

"Well, that's just God damn great! You're a real piece of work. If I was a drug dealer you would be in deep shit right now. Believe me you'd be on someone's hit list. What the fuck were you thinking? I'm packing up and leaving now. My work never mattered for the eight months we've been together, why now has it become such an issue?"

"Why are you so upset? If you aren't a trafficker there should be nothing to worry about. This is the reason I've decided to end our relationship, you are a mystery, I still don't know who you are after being together for over a year, not eight months, genius. Sometimes I watch you while you're sleeping and it seems you never relax; your body is always jerking and twitching. I wonder if you're chasing after butterflies or being chased by some monster, in your dream. When your son Nigel visited at Christmas, he told the story of how all of your children were afraid to wake you from sleeping because you would abruptly jump up with your fists clenched in an aggressive posture. So, they would use a broom handle and poke you from a safe distance then run out of the room. Everyone thought it was hilarious and laughed, except me. I thought it was sad thinking about what would cause someone to react that way. I asked Nigel later that night and he told me about your childhood with your father and your time in prison. Santiago, the reason for me ending our relationship is that I'm falling in love with you. Why I said you have no future is that you seem to live only for the day, for the hour, for the right now. You don't ever talk or make plans for the future or for our future. I feel lost, need some security in my life. Who knows what could happen with the life you lead. You're here one moment and then you vanish in a flash. You could be killed, busted, arrested, or decide to just never come back, leaving me alone. How has anyone ever been able to risk a relationship with you? Oh, that's right they've all given up. Don't you want a mellow life, a safe place, a home with someone who will be there for you, to take care of you, someone to love you?"

"And where could I find such a person? I'm not sure if that type of life is what I want at this time. I did the marriage thing, the house, the eight to five job, the family. I failed miserably at all of it. I'm grateful that my children were able to survive the fiasco, coming through it apparently unscathed. I'm not in favor of doing it all over again. The good side of having made a mistake is that you know when you're doing it for the second time."

"Tell me what it is you are searching for in life. What do you want?"

"What do I want? I want a woman with the faint taste of cocaine on her lips, a dash of peril in her kiss, with laughter that sings like mission bells at midnight, a cool summer breeze in her touch, the smell of a far-off rain in her hair, with skin smooth as a river stone, there's temptation in her smile, a hint of confession in her lies, enticement on her breath, with ocean waves that splash in her eyes, and she can throw a mean punch.

"Get out! Now go, you son of a bitch!" Those were the last words I heard from her.

Remember what I wrote about there never being a right time to say the wrong thing. Guess I should have lied.

"Thanks for picking me up, Johnny. I knew things wouldn't work out with her. It's all for the best. She's got a cousin or uncle who's a captain in the border patrol. Then she tells him about my passports and my travels for the last few years to Mexico and Colombia. And to end it all she called me a 'son of a bitch.' Can you believe that shit?"

"No way? I know your mother was a very nice lady. Maybe you should want me to get rid of her for you? Make the problem go away."

"What the hell is wrong with you, Rico? Have you been watching movies again, *Scarface* or *Blow*? No, I don't want you to do anything to her. You got it?"

"Yo entiendo. But I never like that womens. She always stares at me real strange. She kinda freaked me out. I'm happy you're not with her anymore."

"Where did you get this car? Why aren't you driving the van we used for the run?"

"Well somewhere I lose the keys and the rental guy can't come 'til tomorrow with new keys. So, I borrow this ride from the hotel parking garage."

"You stole this car?"

"No, I borrow it to pick you up!"

"Oh Rico! What am I going to do with you?"

"Why, you wanna do something together?"

The Bare Necessities

I'm confused by drug testing and how they determine the results. I've been subjected to participate in this invasion of my privacy on numerous occasions, always perplexed by their findings. Believe me, I've asked many times what the test is designed to discover. The answer is always the same. "The purpose of the test is to see if there are any drugs in your system."

The drug test results, if they're allowed to disclose them, are presented by someone with an apologetic expression, whispering the findings. "I'm sorry Mister Santiago but you failed. We found marijuana, cocaine, and traces of opioids, possibly heroin or oxycodone in your system. I'm not supposed to share the results of the test, but I'm concerned with your drug use. Do you need help with an addiction? I can arrange an evaluation for you with a drug counselor."

From my first experience with this violation of my civil rights until now, the findings I must confess still leave me flummoxed.

"No thanks, I don't need to be locked up with a bunch of head cases for three months or so. I've already been a passenger aboard that crazy train. Also, I don't have the luxury to take advantage of your offer. I'm sure my parole officer will be determining my agenda for my immediate future. But let me ask you this, if I am being tested for evidence of drugs in my system, wouldn't it be correct that if I test 'positive' I've passed, not failed? Therefore, I object to the results of your test under the pretense your explanation and procedures are deceptive, false, and misleading. I demand my results be documented as 'Pass' and not 'Failed'."

"Ooooo, Mister Santiago you ..."

"Call me Santi."

"Are you an attorney? You're so cute when you get all worked up throwing words around like a Philadelphia lawyer."

"Listen ..."

"Meredith."

"Listen, Meredith, lovely name."

"Named after my grandmother."

"I'm sure she is just as lovely as you."

"She passed away six months ago, cancer. I miss her so much, we were like sisters."

"I felt your pain, saw it in your face the second she was mentioned. It's difficult to express condolences and I don't want to come off as patronizing. Although, I have experienced the deaths of loved ones and would like to offer a bit of advice that comforted me during those trying times."

"Please go ahead." She sits on the sofa next to me in the reception area with just an old codger waiting for his results.

"Think of the wonderful moments you both shared together, the laughter, the hugs, the kisses, and love. She'd want you to embrace those memories, not to mourn her passing. When you think of her and the memory causes you to smile it's a wonderful tribute to her life."

"Who are you Santi? Are you some kind of spiritual healer? What a comforting and sincere way for me to express my emotions. Usually, people begin to express their feelings and pain they've experienced, making the moment about them, completely invalidating my feelings. I'm sorry, but the last thing I want to hear is someone else's story. Is that wrong?"

"No one's pain is greater than your own. I'm not sure who's quote that is but it's not mine."

"Well, it's perfectly fitting for the subject of this conversation," she continues. "Listen, I want to tell you something important. There are instructions on your client sheet to inform Randall Cunningham at the State Corrections and Parole Office of the results of your test. I'm sorry but Mike, the new guy called already. I wasn't supposed to tell you the results of your test but you're such a nice guy."

"Ya, I figured my P.O. would be right on top of this. Don't feel badly, you're just doing your job. This isn't your problem anyway, it's my doing."

"Hold on a minute, I'll take care of this. I know what I can do."

"Don't do anything that will jeopardize your position here. Please don't risk your job for me."

"I'm the office manager, I've got it covered. Don't worry I can't fire myself."

She disappears into the back area. A short time later, two state troopers enter the reception area. There's no doubt in my mind who they're here for. One trooper covers the reception room as the other strolls to the front desk then the testing area calling out for an employee. Meredith materializes from the back and immediately engages the smokey in conversation. I'm unable to hear, but I know what they're discussing and I prepared myself for the consequences, which are my parole being violated and being returned to prison to serve out the rest of my sentence. I begin to question the authenticity of her "grandma story" thinking it may have just been a ploy to keep me occupied until the troopers arrived. They finish their conversation and Meredith points me out to the trooper. He walks directly toward me as his partner grabs at his handcuffs. Meredith has a huge smile on her face, giving me the thumbs up sign.

"You Santiago?" He asks in a John Wayne tone.

"If you're from Publishers Clearing House or State Lottery Office then I'm your man."

His partner finds a bit of humor in my response and chuckles.

"Very funny, you're a real comedian. Now, I'll ask you again and expect a serious answer, no smart mouth. You got it?" He badgers.

"I'm Santiago, officer, how may I help you?" I answer before he's able to ask again.

"Guess you dodged a bullet today. Randall thought for sure you'd drop dirty and he'd violate your parole. Send your sorry ass back to the joint."

"Tell Randall for me I'm sorry to disappoint him. It's a comfort to know he's pulling for me to complete my parole and make it on the outside."

"Ya, well you keep your nose clean and don't give us a reason to have to meet again. You got it convict?"

I didn't want to piss the prick off any more than I already had. I politely bid him and his partner a good afternoon. But I was unable to resist one last comment. "Youz guyz be careful out there."

They acted as though they didn't hear my goodbye and never turned around to acknowledge me.

Meredith returns laughing then slapping my ass with her clipboard.

"We pulled one over on those troopers, didn't we?" She giggles. I'm expecting her to break into a cheerleader routine with all of her jumping around.

"Meredith, I honestly have no words to express my appreciation. I am so grateful for you covering my ass like that. There's no way I can ever repay you for your help. What did you do?"

"I told them there was a mistake. The new guy read the results incorrectly and you actually tested negative."

"So, you mean I passed the test?"

"Ok, you stubborn ass. Yes, you passed and we found no illegal drugs in your system."

"You are an absolute angel, a Goddess!"

I grab her to give her a hug and kiss on the cheek but she pulls me in close and plants a kiss on my lips leaving me wanting more.

"Wow, I wasn't expecting that at all!"

"You can start paying me back by taking me out to dinner tonight. That is of course, if you're not already spoken for. A guy like you probably has a girlfriend, huh?"

"As a matter of fact, I was recently given my walking papers by that supposed girlfriend. Seems my checkered past clashed with her pastel future."

"So, what then, you're nursing a broken heart?"

"I'm not feeling that way at all. I would be delighted to have your company this evening. I'd enjoy spending time with someone other than my temporary roommate. It's a date."

"Wonderful, I've got a roommate too. She's the drug counselor I mentioned earlier. Did you drive here?"

"No, I haven't been certified to reinstate my license."

"That's okay, I can drive. I'm getting ready to close up. Do you mind waiting a half hour or so?"

"That'll be fine, I've got to wait for my buddy Johnny anyway. He's coming to pick me up and like all Colombians including most Central Americans as well, he has no concept of time."

"Great, we're on the same page. Although, I'm a little disappointed you're not grieving over your breakup."

"Why would that be?"

"They say the best way to get over a woman is to get under another one."

"Actually, now that you mention it, I'm feeling devastated and could use some pampering. Although I'd like a chance for us to get to know one another better before taking that step."

"How sweet of you to say that. It was just a joke. Listen, I should tell you that I know more about you than you're aware of. I'll be back in a jiff."

What have I done to deserve this good fortune? Days like this are so rare, I can't recall the last time a favorable occurrence of this magnitude took place. The gods are smiling down on me. I've got a date with an adorable, incredibly stunning woman, who has a great sense of humor. She's also compassionate and kindhearted to top it off. I dodged more than a bullet today, I dodged a hand grenade due to her quick thinking. I'm still astonished by her altruistic act. People don't usually do that kind of thing for me. In fact, I was sure she had set me up. Santiago got duped.

Although there's something causing me to suspect everything isn't quite right. I had to ask myself, why a treasure like Meredith isn't in a relationship, living with someone, or married?

It's a pebble stuck in my mind's shoe, making me uncomfortable. She knows I'm an ex-con and hasn't asked why I was incarcerated. Most women are on the heel toe express with their backsides turned to you at just the mention of the word prison. I could be a pedophile, a thief, a rapist, or a psychopath serial killer. And here she is willfully going on a date with a guy she has no clue to his character. Wait a second, what in the hell was that comment? "I know more about you than you realize." I'm starting to go to my crazy place. There's something amiss and I'm not sure I want to find out what it might turn out to be.

What am I going to do now? I've already committed myself to an evening with her. Now that I think about it, I don't know shit about her. She could be a fucking psychopath murderer, setting me up for the kill. Maybe she 'does' have a boyfriend and they work as a team murdering unsuspecting ex-cons. Some type of sick vendetta taking revenge on them for the crimes they've committed. Stop Santiago, you're really freaking yourself out! Come back, don't go to that place in your mind. I've gotta get outta here.

"Hey Meredith, I'm going to wait outside for my buddy. What about this old guy here? He fell asleep on the couch. He's been waiting a long time."

"No Santiago, he's the night security guard. He'll be fine."

"Okay, I'll be outside."

It's hotter than a sauna outside and I question my decision to leave the air-conditioned office. It's going on five-thirty and the sun appears as though it has reached its pinnacle, stalled in the sky doling out as much burn as possible before quitting time. I take cover under a Palo Verde tree which doesn't provide much cover, but it serves as psychological shade. It doesn't do shit to keep you cool.

It takes a couple of minutes for me to identify the stinging sensation on my legs and lower back. I recognize what's causing the burning sensation. I stand and start brushing my legs with my hands. Then I pull my shirt over my head, without unbuttoning it. I perform the ceremonial spastic dance, accompanied by a song with lyrics of moaning and screaming. "Fucking fire ants, fire ants, attacking me without mercy!" I cry.

Looking down at the boulder I sat on was a mound of dirt right next to it. There were thousands of fire ants crawling around the nest with all of the little bastards preparing to attack. They were staring up at me, taunting me to come closer and make another attempt to invade their territory. My screaming reaches soprano pitch, capturing the attention of the two employees inside. They stare at me jumping around, laughing, and pointing. Not one of the spectators come forward to offer me assistance.

"Fire ants! Fire ants!" I scream.

Finally, the sleepyhead security guy walks out with a bucket of water. "Got into the ants did ya? Those little buggers can do a lot of damage in a short time. Where'd day get'cha at?"

"Pretty much everywhere, but my legs, feet and crotch is where they concentrated their assault. My back as well and a few of the first wave made it up to my neck."

"You talk like an educated feller. You're not from around these parts, are ya?"

"Listen I'd really like to talk with you, but unless you've got some other purpose for that bucket of water could you pour it over me and get these fucking ants off of me?"

"I'll do your back and legs, you'll have to take care of your crotch yourself."

Meredith appears, running out with a fire extinguisher in her hands. Sleepy pours hot water on my back, then my legs, giving instant relief from the onslaught.

"Santiago close your eyes and hold your breath," Meredith screams.

And she begins spraying me with the white powder from the fire extinguisher. You probably won't believe me when I tell you this tidbit of information but it's the first time I've ever been sprayed with a fire extinguisher. The absolute truth.

"Do you know if this will even work?" I squeak.

"Shut up until I'm done. You don't want to be breathing this stuff into your lungs," she commands.

After a couple of minutes I became extremely cold.

"Hey that's enough, that shit is really cold. Stop, I'm freezing and I don't feel any ants on me any longer. Do you see any on me?" I scream.

I'm covered in white powder looking like a Renaissance statue. The white dust has mixed with the water on my body and it's being baked by the sun causing it to harden like plaster.

Then I hear the strangest music, like a movie soundtrack making this catastrophe more surreal than a Fellini film. It was the Seven Dwarfs from Snow White singing *Hi Ho*

I bought a tape of Disney movie songs for my daughter at the swap meet last week. Johnny has become fascinated with the songs, playing the cassette every time we're in the car. Johnny comes running over in a frenzy calling out to me.

"Bigotes, Bigotes, How you catch on fire? You okay? You need hospital?"

"No J.R. I think I'm okay right now. I got into a nest of fire ants and they attacked me."

"I saw Mar-a-Death girl with the fire finisher and thought you are on fire."

"No Johnny, I used it to kill the ants that were biting him. The dust from inside freezes them and it kills them," she responded.

I begin peeling off the hardened plaster in large pieces and 'Sleepy' lends a hand while humming *Hi Ho*.

The employees begin to leave, and they say goodbye to Meredith giggling as they pass.

"What the fuck is going on here. How do you know Meredith? What did you call her? Meg-a-death? I find it incredibly funny but don't know how you came up with the name. And how do you know her?" I ask Johnny.

"I know her because ..."

"Shut up, I'm not finished. And you Meg-a-death lady, when did you meet Mister Rico? Now don't talk all at once. Meg-a-death. I'd rather hear your explanation first so that way I may get the truth without a bunch of embellishment."

"We met here at the Drug Test Center. We have a contract with the state, Johnny was sent here by his parole officer for testing, like you were. He also attended counseling with my roommate, Linda. He shared some things about experiences you two have had. He is quite the storyteller this Mister Rico, the name he claims you gave him."

"Bigotes, please don't be mad at me. I tell them stories about things that happen to us when we are together. They laughed very much and always say tell more. I don't tell of our work, don't worry about that."

"God damnit Rico, can you be any more obvious?"

"No, that part is true he never told us, not even when we asked but I have a pretty good idea," Meredith winks but I don't acknowledge her gesture.

"Johnny my friend, it's a fire extinguisher but fire finisher works just as well. Now I get Meg-a-death. It's Mare-a-dith, Johnny. Your mispronunciation of the Gringo language ends up being humorous once again. I think she has taken a liking to Meg-a-death? Isn't that so?"

"Actually no, I don't especially care for it, but I didn't say anything because I knew it was difficult for him to pronounce so I let it slide."

"So how did I get mixed up in this bizarre affair?"

"It's more my fault than Johnny's. I mentioned that I had to meet this 'Santiago' he talked about. He showed me a couple of pictures of you and I thought you were somewhat good looking."

"Well, I know that's bullshit, because I'm strikingly handsome. My mother told me."

"All mothers tell their sons that. Did your mother lose her glasses?" She giggled.

"Whenever he told us a story, it always included his best friend, Santiago. He spoke about you like you were some kind of god. As far as he was concerned, you could never do anything wrong. You're smart, funny, and look out for him. You'd never let anyone hurt him. You don't criticize or belittle him if he does something wrong. You are the best friend anyone could ask for and you have a heart of gold, but you have a temper like a rattlesnake and you holler like a bear."

"Johnny embellishes quite a bit," I add.

"Don't invalidate his feelings for you. There's one thing he said that really touched my heart."

"What touched your heart?"

"He said he learned about how to be a friend from you."

"Ok this is enough, save it for my eulogy."

"Bigotes, please say you are not mad at me for saying the things I said. She said she wanted to meet you. So, when you told me you had to go to the drug center place I told Meg-a ..., her, you were coming here today. I know you will not like to have a set up kind date. So, we did it in secret."

"Solo bueno carnal. Solo bueno," I tell my friend.

"So, now that we've got this all out in the open, what are we doing here?"

"You go home with Johnny, shower, and change your clothes. I'll pick you up in an hour. I think we should go to the Casino for dinner. They've got a Prime Rib Steak dinner special and then after we can play some Blackjack. How does that sound?"

"Evidently you have already planned the evening, I don't want to disappoint you by changing your plans. I took you for a vegetarian, Meredith, guess I got that one wrong."

"Why, are you a vegetarian, Santi?"

"A vegetarian? No, my dear. Although I do eat them." I'm the only one that laughs. "This sounds like a night I would have suggested, you're amazing."

"Not really. I read your prisoner profile on the prison website where you communicate with people, mostly women. You said you studied Victorian novels, liked blackjack and gambling, and you even told the reason for your incarceration, which is drug trafficking."

"Well, you certainly did your homework." I put out my hand to shake hers. "Hello, my name is Santiago, I'm pleased to make your acquaintance, Heavy Metal Meg-a-death. See you in an hour or so. You have my address on your paperwork." I lean over and give her a kiss on the cheek.

"Okay see you in an hour or so," she sings.

I get into the car with Johnny for the short ride home. He doesn't say a word, I think he may be feeling me out. Checking my attitude before starting a conversation. He slides the tape into the player and the music blares the words from *Bare Necessities*.

"Hey Santi, so you have a good day?" He asks sheepishly.

"Really Johnny? What do ya think? Just more of the same old shit. Why should I expect otherwise?" I give him a playful punch in the arm. Of course, he reacts as if it actually hurt.

The music continues and Baloo sings about strife

"Santiago, do you know what is strife?"

"Do I know what strife is? Yes, I know strife very well. Let me explain."

And with that, Baloo's final line very simply answers the question for me.

Lavatory Lockup

"Who the hell is knocking on the door?" I whisper. "Occupied!" I yell from inside the airplane lavatory.

So, they knock again!

"Did you hear me? I said occupied. Who is it?" I yell a second time.

Then I hear a desperate quiet voice. "Santiago, is me Johnny. Open the door. I need to come in. Come on, open up."

"Are you for real, Johnny? What do you want?" I say while unlocking the lavatory door.

Johnny muscles himself inside the cramped space. He slams the door behind him then he starts pushing the door lock with brute force back and forth a couple of times.

"I can't even get some private time to brush my teeth and change my shirt? What is so fucking urgent that it can't wait until I come out of the lavatory?"

"The guy across from my seat, he keeps staring at me. It's really starting to freak me out."

"What do you want me to do? Ask him what his problem is or what he wants. I don't know. Tell the flight attendant, say he's bothering you. Now get outta here. Go!"

There's another knock at the door.

"What is this a Goddamn convention? Who the fuck is it now? You think maybe it's the guy that's been staring at you? He's stalking you now," I tell him.

"This lavatory is occupied," I answered in a pissed off tone.

"It's Alma, the flight attendant, everything okay in there gentlemen? Two passengers in the lavatory at the same time is frowned upon. One of you is going to have to exit," the flight attendant orders.

"Okay we'll be out in a second," I answer.

"Great Rico, now we're being reprimanded by the flight crew."

"Santi, I need some room please."

"Goddamn it dumbshit, these airplane lavatories are cramped enough for just one person. They're not made for a goddamn crowd. Move over, let me open the door."

"Here I'll do it," Johnny demands.

"Don't pull so hard on the little knob Johnny! Here let me do it, move."

"The slide bar thing won't move. I'm pulling at it real hard."

"Don't force it! You're gonna break it. Let me ..."

Then I hear the sound of metal rattling as it falls down inside the door. Johnny turns around displaying a broken piece of the lock in his hand. "I think it broked, Santiago."

"Gentlemen, you've got to exit the lavatory immediately," the flight attendant orders once again.

"Excuse me but it seems the lock is broken and we can't get the door open. Give me a minute to inspect the damage."

I start squeezing by Johnny who doesn't allow me room to pass. "Hey, give me some space, will you man."

"I have no room to move Santi. I'm all scrunched up with nowhere to go."

I reach over his back forcing him to bend down so I'm able to reach the doorknob but there's nothing there.

"Hello, flight attendant, are you still out there? It appears the door opener is broken and it's stuck in the locked position. Is there any possible way for you to open it from out there?"

"I just tried the emergency release but it's not doing anything. Let me talk to the captain and see if he has any idea how to open it. I'll be right back."

"Great work Johnny, I swear you're an absolute nightmare," I say sarcastically. Johnny frowns with a guilty look still holding the broken piece of the door in his hand. "In the meantime, let's try to get ourselves halfway comfortable. I'm going to move to the back over the toilet. Are you ready? Suck it up Rico."

With the determination and grace of a Brahma Bull, I push myself against his body and manage to squeeze by the tight space.

"Yes, this is better with a little more room I have," he says.

"Johnny, what in the hell did I just hear? Was that a fart? Did you fart?"

He didn't have to answer, the offensive odor answered for him.

"Damn that's disgusting. Did something crawl up your asshole and die?"

"You push so hard on my stomach I have to make a pedo [fart]. Now I am sorry, here comes one more."

Then he lets go with one of the loudest, butt ripping, ass cheek vibrating, farts I've ever heard. It lasts for what seems like thirty seconds and along with it is the most foul odor known to mankind. I covered my face with my shirt, holding my nose but it's still able to assault my olfactory. I begin to gag loudly.

"Damn Johnny! Stop farting pinche cabron."

"Hello gentlemen, everything okay? This is the captain, is someone getting sick?"

"No one is sick, just a reaction to the toilet smell. I have a weak gag reflex, that's all."

"Good to hear. The bad news is that unfortunately the emergency door opener is broken. When we land in Cartagena I'll have maintenance open the door to get you out. Until then you're going to have to make yourselves comfortable. We've got another hour before we land. Good luck."

"You've gotta be kidding me. Don't tell me we have to stay in here until we land? Are you sure there's no possible way to get the door open? Come on. How about I break through the door? It's just plastic, isn't it?

"If you destroy the door you'll have to pay for a new one. I suggest you relax and get comfortable."

"How much would a new door cost, do you think?"

"I'm not sure. Do you want me to find out?"

"That'd be awesome"

"Sit tight, I'll be back in a jiff."

"We're not going anywhere."

I can hear the captain and flight attendant laughing as they walk away. After maybe five minutes there's an announcement on the public address system. "Hello passengers, this is the captain, there's no reason to be alarmed. Everything is just fine. Unfortunately, we have two passengers locked in the back lavatory unable to exit. There's no cause for concern, we'll get them out when we reach our destination. So, relax and enjoy your flight."

I can hear laughter and applause from the passengers. There they are yucking it up at our expense. I can't wait for the day when I find this clusterfuck amusing.

"This has to be one of the worst predicaments I've ever experienced."

"You don't really think that. No inventé [don't make up stuff]. Santiago. We have things happen to us much worse than this. Do you remember when ..."

"Johnny please. I don't want to be reminded of our past dilemmas."

"Okay, I tell you later. So, what do we do now?"

"How the fuck do I know? What am I your entertainment director? Dance an Irish Jig."

"I don't know what that is."

"Nevermind, I was being facetious."

"What does facejesus mean?"

"Johnny, please don't say anything for a while. Please just be quiet."

"Okay, I will not be talking to you for now 'til later. But you should know ..."

"Rico, shut the fuck up!"

"Hey fellas, it's the captain. I got an estimate on the cost of a replacement door with installation. I don't think you're going to want to hear this."

"Lay it on me, captain, oh my captain."

"Maintenance said depending on the damage to the door frame they estimate it could cost somewhere in the neighborhood of eight hundred dollars. And payment must be made when you deplane at the airport in Cartagena, with your credit card. Plus, you'll need to sign a waiver exonerating the airline of any liability."

"Sounds awfully expensive. Not sure about the waiver. I'll have to give my attorney a call when I receive the document. Thanks, let me think on it. I'll let you know in a while. Hey, I need to ask you a professional question."

"Go ahead, I'll try to give you an honest answer."

"Does this type of thing happen often? People getting locked in lavatories on airplanes?"

"It happens more often than you'd think. You fellas aren't the first to fall victim to being locked in a lavatory. Don't worry we won't divulge your names or the incident if you don't want it to become public information."

"Thanks, captain."

"Santiago, are you very much mad at me?"

"Rico, I gave up getting mad at you years ago. Now I just accept what comes with the friendship. Good or fucked up."

"Perdón, no lo hice a propósito [I'm sorry I don't do it on purpose]."

"I know carnal. Sometimes you just can't help yourself. It's just the way it is."

"Hey, I have some coca. You want to do some?"

"Are you crazy man? Do cocaine in this pint size bathroom made for dwarfs? We'll get all wired up with nowhere to go. You know what? Ya, give me a bump."

We both snort a healthy amount of coca and I start to sweat. There doesn't seem to be any ventilation or air conditioning making it more uncomfortable.

"Santi tengo que cargar [I have to shit] very bad. Please let me over there. I can't hold it. It is diarrhea."

"Now you see? I told you not to eat the sushi at the airport. I said it would make you sick. You never take my advice, you hear me, but you just don't listen".

"Please Santi, hurry I'm going to shit my pants. I think maybe I shit some already when I fart."

Reluctantly, I give in to his request and start the awkward inconvenience of changing places.

It stinks so badly my eyes are beginning to water. I put my nose as close as possible into a small crack between the door and frame trying to breathe some fresh air. It doesn't do much to cover up the overwhelming stench of Johnny's exploding diarrhea. The sounds of the act alone are nauseating.

"See Santiago, I shit some little bit in my pants, look!"

"I don't want to look, Johnny. I can't stomach that kind of stuff." Just the thought causes me to start gagging, retching, and dry heaving loudly. I'm sure my convulsive sounds can be heard throughout the entire airplane.

"Are you finished yet? Give the toilet a courtesy flush. Please."

"Okay, I think maybe I finished."

The toilet flushes along with the sound of strong suction.

"Santi help, I'm stuck. I can't get up. The toilet sucked my ass."

"Hello, gentlemen, it's the flight attendant, Alma. Is everything okay in there? I hear the sound of what seems to be someone vomiting. I'm concerned."

I managed to get my dry heaving under control enough to answer. "There's not much ventilation in here and the toilet smells horribly. We're already starting to sweat. Plus, my friend here is becoming claustrophobic. And there was a strong suction when he flushed the toilet. Now his ass is stuck to the toilet seat."

"It will lessen in a short while. Tell him to wait, don't fight it. Just make the best of the situation. I know it's easier said than done."

"Thanks, Alma."

I look over at Johnny and he's gotten free from the toilet's grip. He's standing with his pants pulled down splashing water inside to clean the shit out of them.

"Johnny, let me get by, I need to piss. I'm so fucking coked up the smell in here makes me want to vomit."

I attempt to squeeze past him but he isn't giving me any space to get by. He's actually pushing against me.

"Damn it, cabron, will you give me a little bit of room to pass."

He tries to move but with his pants down around his ankles he ends up doing the penguin shuffle.

"Santiago, I can't move too much with my pants pulled down. Stop for a minute so I can have room to pull them up." As he squats down to pull them up. I see an opportunity to muscle in between him and the wall. I start pushing on his back to get him to move. It causes him to lose his balance and he slams headfirst into the lavatory doors. There's a loud crash as he makes contact and miraculously the doors burst open from the collision. Johnny ends up lying face down in the aisle, his pants still around his ankles with his ass exposed mooning the nearby passengers. Flight attendants are standing in the service area unable to contain their laughter.

"Santiago, why you push so hard like that? Help me to get up will you."

I'm in complete hysterics, unable to control my laughter.

"Do you need help, sir? Are you injured?" A male flight attendant asks, kneeling down next to Johnny.

"Todo bueno. Todo bueno."

"I told you I thought they were having rough sex in there. I was right," he male flight attendant mentions.

"We weren't having sex pendejo. Mentiroso [liar] don't be spreading that meirda [bullshit] around!" Johnny screams at the attendant. "Santiago, will you come over and help me pull up my pants!"

"Okay, here I come."

I pull him up to his feet and notice a large rip in the crotch of his pants but I don't mention it.

"Rico, you got the door open! Good job carnal," I say praising his accomplishment.

"Is everything okay back here? What's going on?" The captain rushes in looking confused.

I think so, captain. It seems they had an accident and fell against the door. They appear to be uninjured," Alma reports.

"We're just fine. I don't think we damaged the door at all. It looks like it is in good condition."

"I don't think you'll be charged for the repair. It looks in pretty good condition, just some minor damage."

"Thanks, captain, I appreciate your assistance. It feels good to be free again," I scream.

"Alma, I think these gentlemen deserve some complimentary cocktails on the airline's tab. How does that sound?"

"It's a wonderful offer. I'll take you up on it. Thank you so very much."

"Santiago, I have to go again. I have the diarrhea," Johnny whispered.

"Go ahead, there's another lavatory available."

"Yes, but I am afraid of getting locked in again. Will you come with me?"

"Are you out of your mind? No way in Hell am I going to share one of these airplane lavatories with you again."

"Sir, I would be happy to assist you if you're feeling unsure about the lavatory doors," the male attendant offers.

"There ya go, Johnny. In the meantime, Alma, I'll have a double scotch on the rocks and some of those cheese crackers if they're available."

"I'll bring it to your seat. Now go relax," Alma tells me.

"Thank you. Good luck, Johnny."

Johnny disappears into another lavatory looking as though he's going to his execution.

God Might Be A Woman

I never could've imagined I'd be where I am at this moment, about to subject myself to this bizarre esoteric ritual. Yet here I am, deep in the Colombian rainforest near Buenavista Putumayo, a short distance from the border of Peru. The jungle is serene with a calm ambience, causing me to feel somewhat uncomfortable. Whenever it seems too quiet, too tranquil, one can easily let their guard down. In my experience, it's often a sign that something is about to go wrong.

At times like this, I always take extra precautions, so of course, I have to question what I'm doing here with Johnny Rico, my partner in pandemonium. He seems a bit apprehensive to participate in this Inga Indian ritual himself, which I find strangely out of character for him. Usually, any event of considerable risk with unfavorable odds, sure to result in an ill-fated end, is a custom-made scenario for him to dive into.

Johnny's nervousness has caught me off guard, especially considering this expedition was originally his own idea. Some woman he'd been involved with had challenged his machismo, announcing to a crowded bar that he didn't have the cojones to take part in the ceremony. Naturally, this was all it took to provoke him into it, but not until he'd roped me in with him as well.

We're waiting on the shaman (aka. brujo or ayahuasquero) to return from foraging for the chacruna and banisteriopsis caapi used to brew up the ayahuasca, or yagé, a psychedelic potion used by the indigenous people of the Amazon. Its potency as an hallucinogen is said to be intense.

"Bigotes," Johnny says, "come with to the pulpería to get some more beer. All we have is water, toilet paper, marijuana, and cigarettes."

"Johnny, what happened to the six pack I bought this morning on the drive here?"

"It got drinked, carnal. You had some didn't you?"

"Oh sure. I drank one fucking beer and of course you drank the other five."

"They was getting warm. I had to drink them."

"I really don't think you should be drinking right now," I attempt to dissuade him.

"You're going to get high enough from the yagé and probably even vomit, get diarrhea, and who knows what else." I know there's no reasoning with him but I continue. "We were told to purge and not to eat or drink anything beforehand."

"Just a couple of beers, Bigotes. I must have to relax, I'm a little nervous, and I don't want to go by myself."

"Rico, stop with your bullshit. With all the shit we've been through together, the narrow escapes, cheating death, staring the devil straight in the face, I've never seen you nervous. Except for once, when you had to go to the dentist for a broken tooth and you passed out in the waiting room. You were more than nervous, you were terrified."

"See, why you have to remember that story? You know la dentista loves to give people pain. They scare me very much, sí. But then you make me watch that movie with running guy where Nazi man drill and pull his teeth. I don't remember name of movie."

"Oh ya, *Marathon Man* with Dustin Hoffman, great movie."

Johnny gives me a punch in my arm and smiles. "You are never to tell no one that story ever! You understand, Bigotes?"

"Johnny, it's already an entry in my book that I'm going to write someday."

"Please Bigotes, let us go get some more beers."

I give in to his request and we start back down the path along the Putumayo River. It's a two-kilometer trek to the pueblo where the bus had originally dropped us off. There's only one large building and it serves as a multi-purpose grocery store, clothing outlet, liquor store, pharmacy, clinic, and post office. It even has a hall in back where church services and other social events are held.

A group of locals are gathered outside as we approach, and Johnny barges his way through to the beer cooler without apologies.

Looking completely out of place are two gringos, standing there appearing confused.

"Hey, excuse me!" the blond kid hollers at me. "Do you speak English?"

"Yes, I'm fluent in English. I was born in Chicago. Why, don't you speak Spanish?"

"No, not very well."

"You mean to tell me you travel to Colombia then into the jungle and don't speak Spanish? So, what travel brochure recommended you take on such an expedition?"

"Ya, I know, it's pretty stupid to not speak the local lingo, but we thought we would be able to get by. Do you know anything about the yagé ceremony and if we might be able to get in on it? My name is Jordy and my friend here is Cal. We're from Provo, Utah but we're not Mormons."

"Hey Jordy, Cal, I'm Santiago. Do you always mention you're not Mormons after declaring you're from Utah? It seems a bit contrite. Anyways, I'll be heading back to the shaman's shack. It's a mile and a half hike through the jungle. I'm just waiting for my friend to return from inside the store."

Just then, Johnny runs up grinning without having purchased anything. "Bigotes, they have the mezcal you like as your favorite! I'm going to buy it for you. We can drink it after the ceremony. I need to borrow some money. Can you lend me one hundred thousand pesos?"

"Buy for me with my money? Of course. Just hurry up, it's going to get dark soon and I don't want to be hiking through the jungle at night."

I hand him some pesos and he runs back inside the pulpería.

"What have you brought as payment to the ayahuasquero?" I ask the Provo Pilgrims.

"You can't just offer up money immediately, it would be considered rude and a display of disrespect."

"We thought we would pay him whatever he charged. We didn't know there were rules. What did you give him?"

"We, well rightfully I, gave him an African bead necklace, a pair of Nike shoes that were a bit large but seemed to satisfy him, and a Swiss Army knife. After that, we offered him about thirty dollars in pesos each. You guys can do your own bargaining. I'm not going to get involved."

"Okay Bigotes," Johnny announces upon his return. "We are ready to be going now. I get some candy for us, too."

"What the hell are you doing?" I holler as he tugs at my backpack.

"I am putting the beer and mezcal in your pack."

"Here, you carry it," I say while taking it off and pushing it at him.

"Okay Bigotes, why you so much mad and holler? I will pay you back the money."

"Johnny, we've known one another for what, eight, nine years? During that time you have never paid me back any of the money I've lent you! Come to think about it, the first time we met in prison, you asked to borrow some bananas and four Ramen soups which you never paid back. There's no way you could ever even pay me back the interest on that."

"So, what is with these gringos?" he asks, conveniently changing the subject. "They're not coming with us! We don't even know these muchachos. Who are you guys?" he says, turning his attention to the Provo Pilgrims.

"I'm Jordy, this is my friend. Cal. Santiago offered to help us get to the shaman's place for the yagé ceremony. Hope it's okay with you, Johnny. That's your name, right?"

"Ya, my name is Johnny. Your friend with you, he doesn't talk?"

"Cal is low key. He's not the talkative type."

"Let's go, children," I finally interject, "before it gets dark and the mosquitoes come out looking for supper. You coming, Rico?"

"Claro, carnal."

As we start back down there trail, there's a loud thunderclap overhead with a crackling flash of lightning. And here I was hoping we wouldn't be hampered by a rainstorm. In the rainforest, it doesn't just drizzle after all. It begins as a deluge, as if the sky itself were sliced open, pouring forth a tsunami-like wave of rain all at once.

Luckily, the dark clouds drift past over a ridge without pissing a drop on us. I consider it a positive omen, a sign that all is well and shall be.

"Hey Jordy," I holler back over my shoulder. "What do they call a person who speaks three languages?"

"I don't know," he replies, "what are they called?"

"They're called trilingual. What do they call a person who speaks two languages?"

"I get it, bilingual, right?" Cal finally speaks up.

"Welcome to the group, Cal. Yes, bilingual is correct. What do they call a person who speaks only one language?"

"Not sure Santiago. What do they call him?"

"An American!"

This gets a laugh out of the group, chuckling as we hike along.

"Bigotes, it is a funny joke," Johnny says. "Did you just invent it?"

"No, it's an old joke someone told me years ago, when I was in Italy."

As we draw closer to the brujo's shack, it smells like someone's out there burning tires. The brujo has begun to cook up the yagé over an open fire. He's using an oil drum cut in half as a cooking pot. He smiles and motions for us to sit on the tree trunks surrounding the fire. He has an assistant with him by the name of

Carmen. She looks to be sixty or so, with a warm smile and a twinkle in her eyes.

As expected, Jordy and Cal look to me for some type of guidance as to how to approach the ayahuasquero.

"Brujo, I found these two wandering about the village, and they asked if they could share in the ceremony. Is it okay with you?"

"What did they bring as an offering in exchange?"

"Well boys, he wants to know what you brought him as a gift for taking part in the ceremony. What do you have? And don't start pulling out money. Save it for last."

"All I have is my watch, a personal progress medallion, and my New Zealand Mission ring," Cal reluctantly answers.

"For a guy that isn't Mormon, you sure have quite a bit of LDS jewelry. And how about you Jordy? Is there anything you would like to gift the shaman? He's sizing you guys up."

"Here's my own watch and medallion. Give it to him."

"It's your gift to give, not mine. You both give him the items, and after he has evaluated their value, then pay him forty dollars each. Be respectful and considerate."

"Okay, thanks Santiago."

Both of them reluctantly hand over their gifts. The brujo holds them up to examine them, shaking his head in disapproval.

"What's going on Santiago?" Jordy asks. "Did we do something wrong?"

"Settle down kids, he's just evaluating your gifts. Relax."

The brujo asks me to tell them he needs something more to seal the deal.

"Okay rookies, now pay the man and smile. Act as though you're sure of yourselves."

He accepts the Provo Pilgrims' payments then informs us that the yagé will be ready in about half an hour. Carmen nods her head in agreement, stoking the fire below with a stick.

Finally, a more serene atmosphere fills the air. It's beginning to get dark as the night stretches its black canopy across the sky. The stars like silver glitter sparkle and flicker while poking holes through heaven's inky cloak.

"Bigotes, where did you put the mota [marijuana]?" Johnny asks. "I can't find it in this backpack with a thousand pockets and zippers."

"Why must I always be the one to keep track of your shit, pendejo? Think, Johnny. I'm aware it may be a difficult concept for you to grasp, but who had the mota last?"

"You are very much, gruñón [grumpy] today. But you always find answers to problems. I remember now, it is in my raincoat pocket. Si mon, here it is!" he declares. "Thanks, Bigotes, I will roll a porro [joint] for us okay? Ojala [hopefully], I have sábanas [rolling papers]? Para seguro yo los tengo!" [For sure I have them!]

Pacified for now, Johnny whistles happily while he rolls a joint.

"Hey, are you guys going to speak Spanish the whole time?" Jordy asks. "We don't understand and would appreciate knowing what's going on." Cal nods silently in agreement.

"First of all," I reply, "what would you Provo Pilgrims have done if you hadn't run into us? Secondly, not to be rude, but I'm not

100

responsible to entertain you LDS lads out here. Lastly, you introduced yourselves on pretense you weren't Mormons. You lied to me, which I find offensive. You assumed I was a bigot. As it turns out, it is you who is the bigot. If you knew me, you would discover I have no animosity toward anyone because of their religion. Just don't preach your gospel to me! Now that we've got that issue out of the way, I believe an apology is in order."

"You're right Santiago," Jordy says. "I'm sorry I misled you."

"Not misled. Lied!'

"Okay, I lied. It won't happen again. We truly appreciate your help. I apologize."

"Me too," Cal adds.

"If I may ask you a question without being intrusive, what is your reason for partaking in this ritual? Have either of you ever used psychedelic drugs before, or even smoked marijuana? It's really none of my concern, I'm just curious why two young innocent lads are interested in this ritual."

Jordy looks at Cal before responding.

"No, we have never done drugs." Cal says. "I got drunk once on Peppermint Schnapps when I was like fourteen."

"I haven't ever done drugs either," Jordy says. "Our reason for doing this ... promise you won't laugh or ridicule us?"

"I give you my word."

"We have read almost everything written about yagé. We've done extensive research and have heard that some people have a spiritual experience during the ceremony. Well, we want to know if there is a God. We're hoping to get an answer or find him, or for him to find us during the ceremony."

Cal looks to Jordy for validation, then they both look back at me, waiting for my reaction.

"Let me tell you Provo Pilgrims something. That has got to be the most rational and sincere explanation for participating in this ritual I've ever heard. I wish you both all the best, hoping you find what you're looking for. During your research, did you happen to come across any mention of the 'Beat' writers having taken part in the ritual?"

"Ya, but I'm not really familiar with those guys."

"William Burroughs and Allan Ginsberg wrote a book together about their experience, *The Yage Letters*. You guys might want to check it out."

"Cool, thanks for not making fun of us."

It is then that the brujo motions for us to follow him inside the hut.

"Here we go children, may the cosmos, or the gods be accepting of our visit into their realm."

There are a few mattresses on the floor, two hammocks, candles, a couple of lanterns, and a large table in the center of the hut with the legs cut short so it is close to the floor. There's also six or so large pails and he hands one to each of us, explaining they are to be used for vomit and/or diarrhea. Then, with a serious expression, he points toward the mattresses and hammocks, saying once you are in your place, you must stay there. No wandering around. If you need something, ask, and he or Carmen will get it for us. He directs us to sit around the table as the twinkle-eyed Carmen enters with a caldron of steaming yagé.

I explain everything in English to Jordy and Cal.

"Ask him why we aren't allowed to walk around?" Jordy suggests.

"No, I won't! This is his ceremony, and he is the ayahuasquero, so it's his circus and he's the ringmaster."

The brujo shushes my diatribe with a finger to his lips. He explains we should be silent, calm, and become at peace with ourselves.

He pours the murky concoction into several glasses that have been cut from the bottoms of beer bottles and begins chanting in a language I'm not familiar with and spreading smoke all around us, burning what I assume to be is sage. Carmen begins singing softly with a beautiful voice. The lyrics describe a young girl that has left her home to search for answers about life and so on, and so on.

The brujo gestures for us to drink, moving his hand back and forth to his mouth.

"I'm not sure about this Santiago," Jordy says. "Are you confident everything is going to be okay?"

"Fuck no! I'm not promising anything, but the uncertainty is the best part of the trip. Listen, I want it understood by everyone right now, I am not your guide, your coach, your lifeline, or your babysitter. Don't burden me with your doubts, your fears, or anything requiring me to assist you with making sense of your reality. I'm here to enjoy the experience myself. Do you understand?"

"Sorry Santiago," Jordy says. "Just feeling a little unsure and frightened I guess."

"I don't know about this," Cal adds. "I've heard people have died from drinking this shit, but ..." Still in mid-sentence, he snatches up the yagé and slams it down in one huge gulp.

"I have to say that was unexpected," I comment.

"Figured if I drank it, Jordy would have to do it too." And then, right on cue, Jordy slams his own yagé as well.

Having seen the boys through, I turn my attention to Johnny.

"You heard what I told them?" I ask. "It applies to you as well."

"Why you need to be so much a mean person? We are friends that take care of each other."

"I'm glad you see it that way. When do you start taking care of me?"

"Salud Bigotes," he says, tapping my glass with his. "You are more than family. I'm lucky to have someone like you for my friend."

We both pour the concoction down our throats. I start to gag a bit from the earthy taste of it, like wood, dirt, and leaves all mixed together with the consistency of 30-weight oil. It was as though I were drinking the very jungle itself.

"Bigotes, that tasted horrible ... It was like my sister's cooking! Well, talvez [maybe] a little better. She is not a good cook. You remember?"

"Yes, I do."

I give my carnal a fist bump as he comes in to give me a hug.

"We will be fine, you think Bigotes?"

"Yes, my carnal, we will be fine. Enjoy yourself, Johnny. I'm here if you need me."

Meanwhile, Jordy and Cal retire to their mattresses near the door, and I take one of the hammocks in the back of the hut.

I close my eyes, telling myself to relax. The brujo sits in the middle of the room, chanting and spreading more sage smoke with some kind of large, colorful feathers.

I estimate thirty, maybe forty-five minutes have passed before I begin to feel the effects of the yagé taking control of my body, commanding my senses to submit, persuading my soul to accept its divine intervention. I was no longer a part of the life I had lived before.

I opened my eyes to get an idea of how everyone else was doing. Knowing my condition, I imagined the others were starting to experience the same intense reactions themselves.

Johnny was on a mattress staring up at the ceiling, rocking back and forth while whispering what sounded like lyrics to a Colombian church hymn. I later found out it was a Doobie Brother's song, *Jesus Is Just Alright* translated into Spanish with incorrect lyrics.

"Johnny, are you doing alright? How do you feel?"

"Santiago, do you believe in living after you die? I just visited the place we go. I'm fine, but I think I am about to vomit."

He can barely grab his bucket before he's throwing up all the beer he'd consumed earlier.

I turn my head to look at the Provo Pilgrims, lying motionless on their mattresses side by side.

"Cal, Jordy, you two keeping it together over there?"

Jordy slowly turns his head and mumbles incoherently.

"Santiago," Cal says, "this is more than I ever could've imagined. I'm doing all I can to hold on, but it's a losing battle. I keep seeing a naked woman walking around. Do you think maybe God is a woman? Have you seen her?"

"I'm seeing my family standing in a circle around me," Jordy whispers. "My grandparents and my brother, my father, Aunt Jocelyn. They all died years ago. This is a strange experience. But I'm not afraid anymore."

"Enjoy yourselves," I tell them as I turn away.

I lie back in the hammock, feeling something like a warm, soft breeze now blowing on my neck. I turn around to see what could possibly be causing this most peculiar sensation.

And there I was, face to face with a panther, standing no more than a few inches before me. It glared at me with its yellow eyes for maybe ten seconds before it began purring, sounding more like a deep, guttural growl. It bared its fangs for a moment and licked its whiskered lips. And then, just as I thought it was about to have me for dinner, it turned and walked away, heading back out into the jungle.

Really feeling the yagé now, l told myself it was just a vision, although I've never been quite sure.

That's when Cal and Jordy both begin vomiting as well. Between the two of them, it's almost like a scene from *The Exorcist*.

Meanwhile, I'd begun to sweat profusely, rivulets cascading down my face. It wasn't long before I too saw the spectral form of a naked woman, beckoning to me with outstretched arms. I wrestle with the web-like hammock, finally freeing myself from its grasp. But just as I've risen to my feet, the stench of shit and vomit in the hut overwhelms me.

I feel a warm sensation in my shorts. Brown liquid running down my legs. There's no way to stop myself from shitting. The smell makes me retch so hard that I too begin puking.

Carmen runs up to me with the pail and places it on the floor in front of me.

I tell the brujo I must go outside to clean myself. He gives me permission, adding that I shouldn't go far. Cal and Jordy ask why I have permission to go outside. I show them my legs and feet, which are now covered in shit, prompting them to recoil in disgust.

Before I leave, I look back to see how Johnny is faring. He appears to be totally immersed in the yagé, still whispering and rocking back and forth.

"Johnny, I just shit myself. I'm going outside to clean up. Back in a few minutes."

He doesn't respond. Carmen motions me forth, a bucket in one hand a lantern in the other.

Once outside, the jungle begins a conversation with me. I can hear the leaves whisper and the movement of every insect. An unkindness of ravens fly just overhead, squawking their evening greetings. Red howler monkeys emit their throaty screams, bidding all a good night.

Carmen taps me on the shoulder, waking me from my trance. She tells me to walk to the river's edge, where she will wash me off with buckets of water. I follow her through the thick foliage toward the river. She stops just short of the water, pushing me back with her hand on my chest.

"Cuidado, hay cocodrilos en el río [Careful, there are crocodiles in the river]."

There's a few large sticks propped up nearby, apparently for the warding off of crocodiles. She hands me the bucket and grabs a stick. Raising the lantern high above her head, she starts slapping at the ground while slowly walking forward.

"Carmen, don't you think there's a better way to get to the river than having to slap at crocodiles with a stick. I'm not so sure ..."

"Cállate bebé, sé lo que estoy hacienda [Shut up you baby, I know what I'm doing]."

After beating the foliage with her stick and throwing several large rocks in the river, so as to spook any potential predators, she motions for me to come forward, ordering me to stand in the river before her. I do as she says and she fills the bucket with water, pouring it down the back of my shorts. I'm thinking it would be much easier just to take my clothes off and dip into the river to get myself clean.

As she repeats the action again, I take off my shorts and throw them on the shore along with my shirt, standing naked in only my sandals. I wander out a bit deeper, sitting down to let the Putumayo River wash away all my filth. The strong current felt extremely relaxing, as though I were in nature's jacuzzi, being massaged by a million tiny hands.

There's a seventy-five cent moon smiling down on me, large enough to light up the night, reflecting back off of the river. I look down and notice that I now am sporting an enormous erection.

Meanwhile, Carmen has begun screaming at me from the riverbank.

"¿Adónde vas? [Where are you going?] Estás siendo arrastrado por el río, vuelve aquí! [You're being swept away by the river, come back here!] Hay pirañas en el profundo! [There are piranhas in the deep!]"

"What???"

It is then I realize I'm being carried down the river. Carmen is running along the bank, screaming at me, but I can hardly hear anything she's saying, the sounds of the rushing water drowning her out.

I can only make out one word, "pirañas", which she repeats over and over again while frantically waving her arms.

By this point, I'm now in the rapids, the current tossing me against boulders and the occasional tree limb.

Wait a minute, I realize in a moment of lucidity, after rapids there is usually a waterfall. Yet there I was, naked, tripping on yagé, being washed down a river and possibly to my imminent demise.

What was that I'd heard Carmen screaming? Something about piranhas? The Putumayo is a tributary of the Amazon, and I'm sure there are piranhas in there.

Fuck the waterfall, I'll most likely be eaten alive before I even get close to the waterfall, either that or crocodiles may savagely rip me apart!

"Santiago, you must fight for your life," I hear a strange woman's voice calling to me. "Get out of the river now!"

"I'm trying but the current is too strong!"

The riverbank rushes past as I flail about helplessly. A fallen log suddenly appears before of me, and with my last bit of strength I am able to grab onto it. Kicking with my feet and paddling with one arm, I fight the river's force as I struggle back towards the riverbank.

"You can't kill me!" I scream to the heavens. "Many before have tried and failed. You're not taking me yet!"

Abruptly I am hit with a beam of light, then another, and another. Flashlights?

"Identify yourself!" a voice demands from somewhere in the darkness.

"Santiago, from the United States," I manage to sputter, still clinging to my log for dear life. "Please, help me out of here!"

Between the lights on the riverbank, I catch a glimpse of the spectral naked woman I'd seen earlier, back in the hut. Once again, she beckons to me with outstretched arms. I doubt I've strength enough to make it to her on my own, but somehow I can feel a gentle force now pushing me along. I can't help but wonder if I'm experiencing a divine intervention of some kind.

Next thing I know, two guys with AK-47s slung over their shoulders are fishing me out of the water. A lantern is lit, illuminating soldiers on the riverbank. An uproar of laughter breaks out among them, echoing through the night without pause. Damn, I was high, with no idea of how long I was in the river or where I even was.

"What's so fucking funny?" I ask the group in English.

"Where are your clothes?" a soldier interrogates in Spanish. "What are you doing in the river at night? Where are you from?"

Another soldier throws a sarape over my shoulders as the laughter finally dies down. They begin talking amongst themselves, apparently unaware that I understood what they were saying.

An officer adorned with gold epaulettes and a red beret approaches me, speaking very poor English.

"Do you speak Spanish?" he asks. "What is why you is here now?"

"Yes, I speak Spanish. I was with the ayahuasquero, el brujo. I drank some yagé and went into the river to clean myself. Then the river sucked me up and took me away."

There came a break in the traffic of my mind, long enough to discern this group now surrounding me. Based on their uniforms, I quickly surmised they weren't the Colombian military but FARC guerrillas, a revolutionary group opposing the current government.

I overheard a couple of soldiers discussing the possibility I may be a spy. Then I heard what I really didn't want to hear.

"We should take the crazy gringo prisoner and hold him for ransom. Maybe his family will pay a lot of money for this crazy pendejo. What do you think, Capitán?"

"Cuál es tu nombre? [What is your name?]", the officer asks.

"My name is Santiago, from Tucson, Arizona," I tell him. "I am here for the yagé ceremony only. If you are thinking about taking me hostage for ransom, let me tell you: There's no one I know who will pay a single peso in exchange for my freedom. Although some of them may offer a small sum for you to hang on to me instead."

The officer laughs as he extends me his hand.

"I'm Captain Arturo Batista of the Revolutionary Armed Forces of Columbia. Pleased to meet you, Mister Santiago."

"The pleasure is mine, Captain."

"I don't think you're a spy, because no spy would risk his life in a river full of crocodiles and piranhas, doing so naked on top of it. I'm surprised you are alive. Did you know there's a 30-meter [90-foot] waterfall just half a kilometer down the river? I believe you when you say no one will pay a ransom for you, because you are so stupid. We know where el brujo lives. I will have my men return you there on one condition. You must not say anything about meeting us here. Do I have your word?"

"Captain, you have my word. I do have one question, though. Did you happen to see a naked woman on the riverbank before I was pulled out of the water?"

"No, there was no one else here. You are seeing a yagé spirit in your mind that is not real. Go with God's blessing. I can't believe you are not dead, you should be more careful. Nos vemos, Santiago."

He smiles and salutes in farewell.

"Thank you for your help. Nos vemos, Captain."

He points to two soldiers and orders them to escort me back to the brujo's shack.

It's pitch black out by this point, darker than I can ever recall the night being. I remember how the moon had shone so brightly before, earlier in the evening.

"Con permiso, muchachos," I ask politely. "How far is the brujo's place? And by any chance did you bring a flashlight? It's very dark and I can't see where I'm going."

The taller of the two walking behind me answers.

"It is maybe four kilometers. We have a flashlight but we only use it in an emergency. We don't want to be found by Colombian military. You will be okay, we know where we are going."

For the first time, I take a closer look at my escorts, noticing they can't be more than fourteen years old. Along the way, the boy soldiers practice their karate on invisible enemies, mimicking famous actors, grunting dramatically as though they were in a movie. I found it quite funny but didn't dare show my amusement. I wasn't sure if they'd get angry, and I didn't want to push my luck.

Meanwhile, the yagé was finally beginning to lose its potency. I was still having hallucinations, however, seeing all manner of things in my peripheral vision along the jungle path. The moon had once again returned to the night sky, lighting our way through the darkness.

As we get closer to the shack, I hear a voice calling from somewhere in the jungle. The soldier boys grab me and push me into the underbrush, ordering me to remain quiet. I hear the voice once again, closer this time, as the muchachos ready their AKs.

"Santiago, adónde está? [where are you?]" the voice echoed through the night. "Santi, answer me!"

"You are Santiago, right?" the tall boy asks. "Do you know who is calling for you?"

"I think it's my friend Johnny. He must be out there looking for me."

"Are you sure?"

The voice called for me again, and this time I was sure it was Johnny. Before too long, we could see the light of his lantern up ahead. I wanted to call out to him, but the boys both shook their heads no.

"You better be dead if I find you," Johnny screams, "because if not I am going to kill you twice! No, three times!"

Glancing back over at the riverbank, I saw the woman once again, the moonlight illuminating her naked body. This time I felt as though she was bestowing a blessing upon me. It wasn't a religious experience, more of an evolution of cosmic consciousness. I wasn't the same person I was yesterday.

"Santiago, you go tell your friend shut up," one of the boys orders. "Be quiet!"

"Okay, thanks for your help."

I look back over at the riverbank one last time, finding the woman now gone. A feeling of vague sadness washes over me, though I am grateful to have reached the end of my ordeal.

"Johnny, you've got to stop screaming," I say as I emerge from the underbrush. "You're waking up the dead!"

"Who said that? Santiago, is that you?"

I step into the light of his lantern and Johnny rushes up to me, hugs me and starts sobbing uncontrollably.

"I thought for sure you were dead, Bigotes. The old witch lady said you were taken by the river. She told us there were crocodiles, piranhas, and a waterfall. She was crying and not making sense, so I didn't know what to do. I waited for some time and then decided to search for you. I took a lantern and started walking down the path by the river. Then something very strange

114

happened. A panther walked up next to me, he stared at my eyes and I could hear him talk inside my head. He said to follow him, he would take me to where you are. So, I follow him for a long while until just before you jump out on me. Did you see him too?"

"My trusted friend, I have seen more than I am able to describe right now. Thanks for coming for me, Johnny. But now that you've found me, you can stop crying now."

"Santi, you are naked with no clothes, why?"

"I'll tell you later. Right now, we need to get back to the shack. Something's up and I don't want to be caught in the middle of it. Come on now, let's go."

When we arrive back at the brujo's place, I see my clothes hanging on a wire line near the fire. I pull them down and put them on all clean and warm. We walk inside together and the brujo breaks out in a huge grin, starts singing and dancing around. Carmen runs over crying, hugging me with incredible strength before slapping me in the face and giving me a sharp reprimand. I notice the Provo Pilgrims are still lying right where I'd left them, appearing sound asleep on their mattresses.

"Johnny, how long have I been missing in action? It doesn't seem to have been a very long time."

"Santiago, you were gone a long while. You went missing maybe 9:00, then I go to look for you at 11:30. I couldn't come sooner because I was very fucked up still.

"What time do you think it is now?"

"I have no watch, el brujo has two or three watches."

I walk over to the brujo, who is still performing his celebratory rites. It takes a minute to get his attention, but when I do, he immediately reaches into his leather bag, retrieving three watches. He hands them all to me and continues his dance, repeating the word "milagro" [miracle], slapping me with palm leaves and wafting that damn smoke in my face.

As I checked all three watches, I noticed one was not working, while the other two both read 2:20. I couldn't have been gone that long. It had seemed to be such a short while, no more than maybe an hour or so. Where the hell was I? Where did I go? That's five whole hours I was unable to account for.

"Santiago, I have to tell you about my time in yagé land. It was something so scary and beautiful at the same time."

"Johnny, it's not that I'm uninterested in your experience, it's just that I'm exhausted and need something to eat and drink first. Hopefully you didn't drink all the water. I need to relax, get my thoughts together, make some kind of sense out of what just happened."

He looks at me with an expression of disappointment upon his incredibly dirty face.

"Johnny, for now I just want to let you know how much I appreciate that you came looking for me. Thank you, my friend."

I grabbed a bottle of water I'd hidden in one of the backpack's pockets, found a mattress near the back of the hut, and drifted off into a much-needed sleep. It wasn't long before I was awakened, however, hearing what sounded like gunfire nearby. It wasn't just a few shots, but repeated automatic gunfire. There had to be a battle taking place and not too far from where we were.

"Johnny, did you hear that gunfire just now?"

He cups a hand to his ear and listens with demonstrated interest.

"Yes, I hear it, Santi. Do you think it is gunfire? Maybe it is fireworks for a celebration."

"At 3:00 in the morning? I don't think so, there's a battle going on right now. It's the FARC guerrillas and Colombian military, I'm almost sure."

The brujo hears the commotion as well, listening from the entrance of the hut. He becomes even more animated than before, crying "viva la revolución!" as he resumes his celebrations once more. He tells us that the Putumayo military base is not far away, and he thinks it is being attacked by FARC revolutionaries.

I don't have the energy to concern myself with revolution. I keep my word, saying nothing about my encounter with the rebels before. Instead, I close my eyes and drift back off to sleep, the sounds of gunfire serving as my lullaby.

As I lie dreaming, events of the night's saga replay again inside my mind. The panther. The river. The moon. But the one part of my odyssey I keep coming back to was the beautiful naked woman who'd guided me back to safety.

God just might be a woman!

Johnny's Junk In The Trunk

"Yep Johnny, that's a dead body alright. Now tell me, and it better be good, why in the hell you drive over to my place at 11:00 at night and drag me outside to look at a dead body in the trunk of your car? Wait, this isn't your car. Did you steal a car with a dead body in the trunk? Do you know who your unfortunate passenger is in the trunk? Nevermind, I don't want to know. Turn off the flashlight and close the trunk. Do you want everyone to see what's inside?"

"Santiago, I need your help."

"What have you gotten yourself into now J. R.?"

He slams the trunk and starts bawling.

"First stash the car around back, then come on inside, let me get rid of my company and we'll get this worked out."

His crying is at a critical level, he's unable to catch his breath. I have never seen him so distressed. His entire body is shaking uncontrollably, his arms wrapped around his chest hugging himself. "Santiago, I don't know what to do."

"Hold on, take it easy carnal. Let me tell Katia I've got to cancel our date for tonight."

I inform my guest that I won't be able to enjoy her company. I have a situation that must be addressed. She puts out her hand motioning for some money. We didn't have sex, but I pay her, which is customary.

"Gracias bebé." She kisses me and slaps my ass.

"Buenas Rico, are you okay?" She asks Johnny when he walks in but he doesn't answer.

"Santiago call me the next time you want to pay to not have sex." She laughs and waves as she walks out the door.

"I'm sorry I ruin your good time, Santiago. Thank you for helping me with my problem," he says in between sobbing.

"Okay, first of all, do you need a beer, coffee, or anything?"

"I would like a beer very much. What kind is it you have?"

"What? I don't think you're in any position to be choosy right now. Go get it yourself. I need to get out of this robe and put some clothes on."

I get back to the living room and Johnny is walking around my sofa talking to himself not even noticing I've entered the room. He's on a course to a complete mental breakdown.

"Carnal, come sit down and relax for a while. I need to ask, is anyone going to come looking for you?" I inquire further. "The police or the cartel aren't involved in this in any way, are they?"

"No, no, no. We can talk. No one is looking for me."

"Okay then, let's start with when you left your house tonight. What time did you leave?"

He begins telling me the events leading up to his visit here. "I walk to Chi Chi's bar because it is close to my place at around 7:30. I'm having a beer and watching Futbol on the tele when Danielo comes to sit down next to me."

"Ya, okay I know who he is, there's something I was told concerning him. I can't think of it right now, go ahead."

"He start talking about wanting some cocaine. He wants to get a quarter kilo and shows me a big wad of money that he has. Then he wants to know if I know someone and how much it will cost."

"Okay, it seemed like a bad idea so of course you said yes."

"Yes so, I say yes I will call my guy and let Danielo know tomorrow. But he say no he wants it tonight. So, I say okay to give me an hour to make some calls and get it together. First, I call Michy, but he went to the playa [beach] for the weekend. Then I tried your Mexican friend, Zefferino, but nobody answered. I think maybe to call ..."

"No Johnny, I don't want to hear that you called Chutta!"

"Yes, I call him and he say he not want to talk on the phone and would meet me in fifteen minutes at the bar. And also, no strange faces."

"What did I tell you about that fucking Escobar wannabe? I told you not to deal with him. He's a fucking psychopath and a captain or some bullshit in a gang."

"So, I meet Chutta outside the bar and he tells me how much it will cost. He asked if it was for me and I tell him no it is for Danielo."

"So, what did he say?"

"He said he didn't like him and think he is a police informer. I told him I didn't know. Also, to meet him at the old mission at 9:30 and have all the money."

"Johnny, you should have called me right then."

"You said you didn't want to hear or see me for a week because you were mad at me again. So, I didn't call you. I forgot why you were mad at me."

"You forgot to pick me up from the airport and I had to take a taxi with a suitcase full of money and luckily I wasn't ripped off. Sorry did I hurt your feelings? Now let's get back to the problem at hand."

"Thank you for saying you're sorry."

"I wasn't apologizing, Johnny." I continued, "Now come to think of it, someone mentioned to me a couple of months ago that Danielo might be police. I'm sure I would've told you. Don't you remember?"

"Yes, but you say, you think maybe he is an informer. You didn't say for sure you know that he is a narc, so I trusted it was okay."

"What are you thinking? That's the worst logic I've ever heard."

"What is logic, Santi?"

"Something you obviously will never understand. So, I have to ask, is it Danielo in the trunk?

"No, it is not him. Please, don't interrupt Santi," Johnny continued to explain with an occasional whimper, "Danielo agreed to the price and told him he would call his cousin Rafael to drive us to the mission for the cocaine deal. I knew Rafael from when he worked as a guard at the prison in Bogota. Danielo introduced him to me a couple months ago. He recognized me from when I did time there and told me he quit because it was too dangerous. I'm sure it was so, every convict in the joint wanted to kill him. He was a mean Son of a Bitch that enjoyed beating the shit out of prisoners with a piece of iron rebar. He caused a lot of broken bones and cracked skulls."

Johnny continues while walking to the refrigerator for another beer. Rafael showed up at the bar at 8:45 to drive them to the location of the dope deal. He tells me he was not feeling good about doing the deal but knew it was too late to call it off. He tried to explain to Rafael his connection didn't want any strangers there. But he yelled at Johnny that he doesn't trust anybody and some of the money was his and he's not going to let anybody rip him off.

"We start driving to the mission and I still have a very bad feeling." He continued to explain, "They both have guns and pull them out and tuck them into their waist when we get close. When we pull off the main road into the driveway ..."

Johnny stops talking and puts his head in his hands. He takes a deep breath and starts once again. Rafael started barking orders at Johnny adding to the tension that was building as they reached the mission. He parked the car close to the front entrance. Once again, he started giving orders, telling Danielo to wait in the car, he and Johnny would handle business. Johnny worked up the nerve to tell Rafa he didn't like him giving orders and told Rafa to give him the money. He slaps the cash into Johnny's hand.

"Stop for a minute, I need to count the money to make sure it's all here," Johnny tells Rafa.

Suddenly like a shadow from hell, Chutta appeared with a pistol on his hip and two muchachos with flashlights and machine guns for backup.

"What did I tell you, Rico? I said no new faces," Chutta says.

"I'm sorry, I told him you didn't want any strangers. He wouldn't listen."

"And of all the assholes in the world you bring this pendejo."

Johnny stops talking, stands up and has an expression of extreme terror on his face.

"Rafael started to walk toward Chutta and took out his gun, I think to give to Chutta so there would be no gun play. And put out his other hand to shake. With no warning someone come up from behind and shot Rafael in the back of his head!"

"You must have been terrified, you were thinking you were next."

"Carnal, can you not talk and stop me from telling the story?"

"Sorry, go ahead, shoot."

"You are not funny with your joke! So, I think maybe I am next, but Chutta walks to me and shakes my hand."

He assured Johnny nothing was going to happen to him. He explained that Rafa beat his brother and cousin when they were in prison. His cousin died from the beatings. He told Johnny that Rafael was now a "Sapo" [snitch] for Metro Police.

"See what did I tell you about Chutta, he is a fucking psychopath."

"Then I hear more shooting outside," he begins again, "They are shooting at Danielo who runs away from the car. I don't know what happened to him."

"Jesus Christ Johnny, you must've been freaking out."

"Yes, I was very scared. Then Chutta and another guy put Rafa's body in the trunk of the car and told me to get rid of it. He also said to tell you, hello."

"Well, wasn't that nice of him."

" Next, I don't know what to do. Then I think of my best friend in all the world and I come here to you."

"Okay Johnny, no need to blow smoke up my ass. I'll help you but you're going to owe me big time."

"I don't care, just want this to be over. I still have all money, here I will give it to you I don't want it."

He hands me a large wad of bills with a red rubber band holding it together. His hands are still shaking and there's tears running down his face.

"What ideas do you have to take care of this?"

"First of all, thanks for the cash. I'll put some away for you."

"No, I don't want any of it, you keep it."

"You say that now, but tomorrow you'll be telling me what a horrible friend I am to keep all of the money."

"What are we going to do Santi?"

"You need to stop crying and shaking. You look like you've been crying all day. Your eyes are red and you've got bags under them. I want you to go back to the bar and have a couple drinks. If anyone asks why you've been crying, tell them your cat died."

"But Santi, I never have a cat."

"For Christ's sake, it's a lie. An excuse for why you look like you've been bawling for hours. I'm going to drive the car over to Barrio Magdalena, leave the doors unlocked and the keys in the ignition. The car won't last more than five minutes in that neighborhood. It'll get stolen and it will become someone else's problem. Maybe the policía will arrest whoever is driving it.

124

"Santiago, do you think your plan will work?"

"I'm sure of it. Now let's get outta here and take care of business."

I drive Johnny back to the bar instructing him not to say anything. Then I repeated, don't say anything. Wait for me to come back, don't go anywhere. Stay at the bar. He said he understood. He would be quiet and not talk with anyone.

I was nervous driving to Barrio Magdalena in Rafael's car with his body in the trunk. I questioned my decision to participate in another Rico fiasco. For some strange reason I smile, I'm turning pages of memories in my mind of adventurous mayhem we've encountered. Out of the entire population in this fucked up world, I can't think of anyone else I'd rather have as a friend. Every bizarre situation we've experienced together has been worth any penalty we've had to pay.

I reach the barrio and cruise the streets looking for the perfect place to dump the car. There's an all-night grocery store with a few cars parked in the lot. Across the street is a bar with a bunch of ominous looking vatos hanging out in the front. I park the car next to a couple of other cars near the side of the building. I get out and leave the motor running, the lights on, and keys in the ignition. I trot into the store making it appear I'm in a hurry. Once inside, I notice a small restaurant and take a seat. After looking at the menu for a couple of minutes, I ordered a cheese empanada and Coca-Cola to go.

When I get my order, I look at my watch and see that close to ten minutes has passed. I figured it should be enough time for the car to be stolen.

I slowly walk toward the front entrance to see if the car is in the parking lot. Just as I had hoped, it had mysteriously vanished. I don't react to the car's disappearance. I walk to the street with a fair amount of traffic and hailed a taxi.

I arrive back at Chi Chi's Bar and of course Johnny is nowhere in sight. I walk around searching for his sorry ass, checking the bathroom and the outside beer garden in back but no Johnny. Damn it, I can't believe he's unable to follow simple instructions. I turn to leave and he strolls in looking like he's carrying the weight of the world on his shoulders.

"What the hell is wrong with you Rico, didn't you understand what I said?"

"Oh yes, I understand very well your instructions. But Chutta came by looking for me to give a present. It is a big surprise."

"What kind of surprise?"

"Come outside I will show you."

We walked to the far end of the parking lot. Johnny stops and points. "This is the surprise. Chutta brought it here for me."

"Son of a Bitch. What the fuck is going on?" I scream in anger.

Sitting in the back of the lot in the darkness was Rafael's car. The same car I had just disposed of an hour ago.

Johnny explains that Chutta was extremely pissed off and hit him a couple of times. The thieves that stole the car brought it to Chutta to try to sell it. He wanted to know how it was stolen from me. I didn't know what to say, so I told him you were getting rid of the car and I have not heard back from you. Something must have gone wrong.

"Chutta said nothing better go wrong again or I will be sharing the trunk with Rafael," Johnny whimpers.

"Can you believe this shit? What fucking horrible luck. The car gets stolen and brought straight back to that little punk." I'm in total disbelief at this point. "Okay, let me think for a minute. I need a drink to settle down."

"I think a few drinks," Johnny adds.

We take a seat at a table and a cute waitress comes over to take our order. She smiles at Johnny, and he starts flirting with her attempting to get familiar.

"Are you for real? We are in the middle of a possible life or death situation and you're flirting with a waitress? Of course, you are, why should this be any different than the number of times we've stood face to face staring into the eyes of death." I slap him on the back of his head and he starts crying again.

"Why you hit me Santi? I was just being nice."

"Ya, I'm sure. Listen, here's an idea. What about the automobile junkyard? Do you still have an uncle that works there? Remember the guy with one arm and laughs crazy like all the time."

"You mean my mother's brother, Oscar?"

"I don't know his name. Ya, I guess, crazy Oscar."

"No, he was killed last year, he was hit by a train. Hey Santiago, how about maybe we just drive it off the pier into the bay? It will be very easy."

"Everybody dumps cars and bodies into the bay. It's so unoriginal plus the police probably watching. No, that's not a good idea. Damn it, there I was earlier ready to get laid by a gorgeous woman then what? Suddenly a Rico clusterfuck bites me in the ass."

"Santiago you are now being a prick. If you don't want to help then go away."

"I don't like the tone in your voice, Rico. You're adding to my stress making stupid comments."

"I am thinking about Danielo. If he's still alive he might go to the policía and tell them."

"He doesn't know Rafa is dead. This is getting more than I can handle. I'm too old for this shit, Rico."

"Bigotes, you've been saying you are too old for five or six years now whenever we have a problem. but no matter how old you get, we always find a way to make it go away."

"I've got it! We can stash the car in the garage at your sister's house. I'll give her some money to keep her happy. That'll buy us some time. Then we'll have a better idea of what we're facing and take care of this mess tomorrow night. Sound good carnal?"

"Yes, it sound real good. Let's go!"

We leave the bar and Johnny frantically begins searching his pockets for what I assumed were the keys.

"No, Johnny, I don't want to hear you can't find the keys."

"Santi, I don't think he give them to me. He ... oh yes he leave them in the car for me, I remember now."

We get to where the car was parked earlier and it has vanished, disappeared, fucking gone. Nowhere in sight.

"God Dammit Johnny! This is turning into a fucking nightmare. Where in the hell did the car go? Who do you think stole it? Ya know what? I don't fucking care. I'm done, finished with this pain in the ass Rico quagmire.

"*Gagmire* is good thing or bad thing Santiago?"

"What do you think Rico?"

"When you call me Rico, I know you are angry and pissed off. But it is not my fault. The spirits are not helping us right now. What should we do? Chutta is going to kill me if he finds out."

Then as though there was actually a merciful God, Rafael's car pulls up to the curb and the driver beeps the horn then yells to us, "Johnny, Santiago, what's going on? I've been looking for you Rico." It's Danielo, driving the car.

"We've been searching for you. I thought maybe you were dead," Johnny says in a sincere voice.

"Where is Rafael? What happened at the Mission? Those pinches tried to kill me."

We walked over to talk to him. I wasn't sure how to handle the situation or what to say.

"Johnny let me do the talking, don't say a word," I whispered.

"They started shooting at me. I ran into the jungle and hid out until they left. I walked all the way back and saw Rafael's car here with the keys inside. I looked in the bar and didn't see him. The bartender hasn't seen him either. Do you know what's happening?"

"Danielo, pull the car in and park it and I'll explain what happened," I said.

He pulls the car into the parking lot and gets out. He's filthy, his clothes are full of mud as well as his hair and face. Even in the partial light you can see the mosquito bites on his arms. He's full of red bumps and he's furiously scratching everywhere on his body.

"What do you think happened?" Danielo asks.

"I don't know how to tell you what went down. But it's not good news. Johnny told me what happened and he's too upset to talk about it." I began my version of the incident.

"When they got to the mission, Chutta was pissed off that Johnny brought Rafael with him. Rafael started to argue with Chutta calling him a pendejo [asshole] and a ladron [thief]. Chutta started toward Rafael and he pulled out a gun. One of the gang members walked up behind Rafael and shot him in the head. They put his body in the trunk and told Johnny not to go to the police or he would be sharing the trunk with Rafael. Johnny drove to my place, then we came looking for you. We asked if anyone had seen you but everyone said no. We didn't have your phone number and no one else had it either. Tell you the truth, we thought you were dead."

Danielo didn't seem to be upset with the news. There's no expression of grief or sadness on his face. "I always knew he would get whacked someday. I think he killed Chutta's brother in prison and I told him it was a bad idea for him to take part in the drug deal. He never listened to anyone else all of his life."

"I'm sorry for you Danielo." Johnny walks over and gives him a hug.

"What do you think I should do?" Danielo asks me.

"I wouldn't go to the police. There'd be a lot of questions and an investigation. I think you'd be next on Chutta's list," I answer.

"Maybe you should just drive the car into the bay and forget this ever happened," Johnny instructs. He's got some kind of obsession with dumping the car in the bay. I wonder how many times he has done it before. He seems pretty confident about doing it that way.

"No, I want to keep the car. I can say he sold it to me and he left for the United States. But I don't know where we can dump his body. You guys have any ideas?"

"What do you mean we, jefe? How did I get dragged into this made for T.V. disaster movie? I told Johnny from the get-go I didn't want any part of this," I explained.

"Wait Santi, you remember the fat kid with glasses that you helped when some guys were beating him, trying to rob him. I don't remember his name. But he said if there was anything he could do to pay you back just ask. Remember?"

"Ya, I remember. He's called Gafas. So, what does that have to do with ... Oh Johnny you're a genius. You found a solution to the problem. He's a garbage man and drives a truck emptying dumpsters. We can throw the body in a dumpster, he empties it at the dump and it gets buried with the other garbage. What do you think, Danielo?"

"I like it. How do you get a hold of this guy?"

"He should be working now, it's almost 2:00 am. Let's drive around until we see a garbage truck and we'll ask him to get a hold of Gafas."

"It is Saturday and the truck gets garbage in my neighborhood. Let's wait over there we will see a garbage truck." Johnny says with confidence.

We get to the car and Johnny jumps in the back seat Danielo walks to the passenger side door, opens it then slides in. They obviously aren't interested in driving and somehow I've been elected.

"So, tell me, how did I get chosen to be driver?"

Neither of them respond and pretend to be preoccupied with other pressing matters. I turn the key and the engine purrs but notice the gas gauge is buried under the 'E'. I want to comment on neglecting such an important matter but it would only add to making the situation more tense than it already was, so I let it slide. "We've got to hit a gas station as soon as possible. The gas gauge arrow is past the 'E'. Hope you've got money to pay for the gas?" I say to Danielo.

"I've got a few Pesos. Most of my money was in the cocaine fund. What happened to the money, Johnny?"

I was hoping Johnny wouldn't go soft and tell Danielo he had the money and would give it back. After all, we've been out most of the night risking our asses to do someone else's dirty work. We're driving around with a dead body in the trunk of a car that isn't ours. Our lives have been threatened by a high-ranking Colombian gang member to dispose of a body so it will never be discovered.

"I don't have any idea, Danielo. He gave it to me to count then quickly grabbed the cash from me when I had finished. I don't know what happened to it after Rafa was killed. I was more worried about getting out of there alive. I'm sure Chutta took the money."

Good form Rico, you make me proud.

We find a station that's open and donate some pesos for gas but Johnny informs me that he doesn't have any money. They both

132

sit in the car making no effort to help me with paying or pumping the gas.

"So, you think there's an attendant that'll come out and pump the gas?" I say in a sarcastic tone.

"No, I think you've got to pump it yourself," Danielo says.

"I'll go inside and pay but one of you lazy carepiches [Costa Rican word for Dick Face] will have to pump the gas. I'm not your chauffeur. So, somebody get pumping."

I head inside to pay for the gas and as I walk back I notice neither of the pinches are pumping the petrol.

"What is wrong with you cabrons [dumbasses]? I'm not going to pump the gas. Do you hear me?" I holler.

"Santi, Danielo tell me to do it. He no ask, he ordered me like he's my boss. So, I tell him to go to hell, he should do it because it is all his fault what happened tonight," Johnny says.

Then Danielo turns toward Johnny and starts throwing punches stretching over the seat to reach him in the back. Suddenly with one perfectly placed punch, Johnny knocks out Danielo. He's down for the count.

"I'm sorry Santi, but he attacked me. I had to hit him."

"Perfectly okay with me. Just wish I had a camera, that was so damn funny. I'll pump the gas, just relax. You've been to hell and back tonight." I start laughing.

I start to pull out into the street and I stop to let a garbage truck get by. The truck pulls up to the dumpsters on the side and begins emptying the first of three .

"Santi there is garbage truck. You want me to talk to him?"

"No, Johnny, I'll take care of it, but come with me."

I park the car and Johnny and I walk over to the truck. I wave at the driver and he beeps his horn.

"Senior Santiago, how are you. It has been a long time since I've seen you." He yells out his window.

"Hello Gafas, yes it has. I need a favor. Can you come down so we can talk?"

He opens his door and jumps down, leaving the dumpster in the air. I explain our predicament and ask for his help. Without any hesitation he says yes, no problem. I give him a hundred dollars which he refuses but I insist he accept my offer. He thanks me and begins instructing us how we should take care of our package.

"There's dumpsters behind the hospital that are always full. They're also very well hidden where nobody will be able to see you depositing your garbage. It is my next stop so head there now. Be careful. Good to see you again and I don't know anything."

"You're a god, Gafas. Now I owe you."

We run to the car and Danielo is awake and holding his hands over his nose.

"Welcome back, Sleeping Beauty, we're ready to rock n' roll. Got it all worked out," I tell him all excited.

"What's the plan?"

"You'll see."

It takes ten minutes or so for us to reach the hospital. I cruise the alley searching for the dumpsters. They're well concealed like he said because I can't seem to find them. I turn into what I think is a parking lot and there they were, lined up and well hidden. I pulled the car to the side of a dumpster and turned off the lights.

"Okay girls, let's do this. And I'll need both of you to help. No fighting until we are done. Understand?"

They both exit the car and they stand at the trunk while I fumble with the keys to find the one to open it. After a minute, I find the right key.

"Okay, come on, each of you grab the body and the three of us will throw it in the dumpster. Ready, one, two, three, lift!"

"Santi, he is too long and he won't bend so we can't get him out," Johnny says. Rigor mortis has set in and the body is as stiff as a tree trunk.

"Of course, of course why should it be any different. It's never easy," I complain.

Then I hear bones cracking and see Danielo bending the body, then he pushes the body out of the trunk. Johnny grabs hold and before I get a chance to help, they throw the body in the dumpster.

"Good job boys, let's get outta here!"

We jump in the car and I head for the main street. On our way we pass Gafas and he gives us a short toot on his horn.

"That's it! We did it! We just experienced an adventure that we'll most likely never be able to talk about. As a matter of fact, I suggest that no one ever tell anyone about this night. Now, I think Johnny and I are going to stay at a hotel tonight, just to be safe. Okay with you J.R.?"

"Good idea, Santi."

I drove to one of my favorite hotels and Johnny and I bid Danielo a good night. I get us a suite and order breakfast from room service.

"What an incredible night, another story for my book. What do you think Johnny?"

"Yes, and I thank you for your help once again. Also, I must tell you something, I have this package I picked up from the ground at the mission when they were putting Rafa's body in the trunk."

Johnny pulls out a bag from his pants and it's the cocaine from the deal gone awry.

"Johnny, you devious, wonderful swindler. I'm in total awe of your actions tonight. We deserve to party like frat boys on spring break. What do you say carnal?" I scream.

"Yes, okay. I have not seen you so happy in a good mood for a long time, it makes me happy too. Can we get some womens?"

"Anything you want! I love you Johnny!" I hollered.

Peyote, Toads, and the Medicine Man

Johnny and I were in Bisbee, Arizona at the house of Screaming Crow (Larry) a Navajo we've known since we shared a cell at a Gray Bar Hotel in El Paso a few years ago. He became one of our first clients when Johnny and I went into business for ourselves. Johnny decided Crow had earned fronting privileges [credit] a practice I've never approved of but Johnny convinced me it's good business.

His theory is when you extend credit to a customer, in most cases they usually purchase more product than they would buy in an upfront cash transaction. Gotta give it to my partner, he was on the money with his assessment of extending credit. I didn't approve of him being so generous with offering the privilege. Screaming Crow has yet to default on our credit terms.

However, that's not the case for a couple of other past clients that turned out to be deadbeats. There's one that still owes us three grand for close to a year. Johnny suggested stealing his Porsche, drive it over the border into Mexico and sell it there. This prick has been granted two extensions to pay his debt. He ignored the deadlines without receiving any penalty for being delinquent with his payment. Johnny was so excited when I mentioned last week that his debt comes due again in ten days. This is absolutely our last request for payment, no more extensions. Johnny has been very creative in thinking of punishments if the debtor fails to settle up. Besides car theft, he's mentioned killing the debtor's dog and of course killing it twice, raping his girlfriend, who I believe he has already banged last December when this deadbeat was doing time in the county jail. He talked about burning down his house even though he found out the house is owned by an Air Force Colonel stationed in Sierra Vista. Johnny's threats will never happen because he is actually a decent person and has a kind heart until you fuck him over.

I was upset with Screaming Crow because someone I didn't know was there while we were doing business.

"He's cool Santiago, trust me. Emmett is the Medicine Man for the Chiricahua Apache tribe and he's my mother's boyfriend, too. He just turned me on to some ass kicking Peyote buttons. Do you want a couple?"

"Larry, you know ..."

He interrupted me and looked pissed off.

"My name is Screaming Crow, don't disrespect me like that."

"It's a bitch when somebody disrespects you, isn't it? You know the rules and disrespected me by not following them. As far as trusting you, I don't trust myself most of the time. How can I trust you? The only person I trust in this entire world is Rico."

"If you want I will go. I'm sorry to piss you off," Emmett offered while standing up.

"It's got nothing to do with you, Emmett. You're just an innocent bystander. You don't have to go. The reason for our visit has already been divulged," I said in a disgusted tone.

"Santiago, why you have to be so much like a prick? We have been knowing Screaming Crow for a long time. He would not never rat us out. Also, he is a good customer. Now you should stop being a grunion [crabby person]."

"Okay Johnny," I agreed.

"Don't let this become a habit, Screaming Crow. Emmett, I apologize for my manners. Once again, I have no hard feelings concerning you. As a matter of fact, I'm interested in talking to you about your people, their myths and legends, and the part you play in the community."

"We are going to do some Peyote tonight at Cochise Stronghold in the Dragoon Mountains and make contact with the spirits of our ancestors. Would you like to come and be a part of the ceremony?"

"Are you serious? I'd be more than honored to attend."

"We can talk then about my tribe. Have you eaten Peyote before Santiago?"

"Yes, I have, quite a few times. I'm very familiar with psychedelics. I'll be just fine. No reason to be concerned about me. Johnny and I have also participated in an Ayahuasca ceremony as well in Colombia. We'll be just fine. Isn't that right Rico?"

"When did you hear me say I was going to do the Peyotes? You just think I am going to do what you do? If you jump over a ditch I am supposed to jump too?"

"Oh Johnny, please, I'm sorry for laughing when you are trying to be so serious."

"Tell me then why you laugh at me?"

"The saying is. If he jumped off a bridge would you jump too?"

"Why would you jump off a bridge? You might kill yourself. That is a stupid saying."

"I'll explain later Rico. Let's finish up here Screaming Crow and take care of business. We've got an appointment in Tucson but it should only take an hour, maybe two at the most. We should be back close to 5:00, long before it gets dark. Would that work for you guys?"

"That'll be just fine, Santiago. We're going to meet Screaming Crow's mother, my partner, his uncle, and a few cousins at Cochise Stronghold. There will also be a couple of people from my tribe. If you are not back by 5:00 we will leave without you," Emmett instructs.

Johnny and I hopped in the pickup after taking care of business with Screaming Crow.

It's only ninety-five miles to Tucson from Bisbee. We would be there in an hour and a half or so. Thirty minutes to make the delivery, then we'd head back to Bisbee. We left at twelve-thirty so if everything goes according to plan we should return by four o'clock or so.

"Hey Johnny, so you're not coming to the Peyote Ceremony tonight? Why not?"

"I will maybe end up going with you but I'm not sure I want to eat the Peyotes. I don't want to get all out of my mind with a bunch of people I don't know. When I'm *Psychodildosized* I have to hold on to myself so I not float away to the magic heaven and maybe not find a way to come back. Do you know what I mean?"

"I understand carnal. There are moments when you go to a place where you don't want to be. If you decide not to come you can probably stay at Screaming Crow's house for the night. I'll leave the pickup with you but don't go cruising around town. There's still twelve kilos of cocaine packed away inside. Tomorrow night we've gotta be in San Diego to take care of Los Sureños."

"You won't be mad with me if I not go to the Peyotes *saramoane*?"

140

"Not at all Johnny. You're old enough to make your own decisions. I'm not an Army Officer or your boss, father or wife telling you what to do. I'm your friend. I will always look out for you and watch your back. You know that, don't you?"

"Yes, but it is good to hear you speak the words. Now I want to cry," he jokes with a chuckle.

"But, listen to me. I do need to say something to you, so remember this. Don't you ever reprimand me in front of a connection again. Do you understand?"

"What is *repurtan*, Santi?"

"It means don't jump down my throat and tell me how to act or correct me in front of a client. Crow broke the rules and disrespected us."

"Okay Santi. I will never do it again."

We reached Tucson without incident but our contact wasn't home. His wife said he was most likely at Érmanos Bar on South Fourth Avenue and it wouldn't do any good to call because they always say he's not there. He knew the meet up was at 2:00 and there's nothing that pisses me off more than a connection being late or having to chase him down. I parked the truck in his driveway and we waited for 25 minutes.

I decided to leave and come back later. Just as I started to pull out of the driveway, Fish Eye [Javier] drives up with his partner Carlos. He starts laying on his horn with long beeps. Instantly, I became upset with him for drawing all kinds of attention to us. His neighbors were looking out their windows with others standing on their porches to see what all the ruckus was about. This type of shit causes me to get stressed out because of the attention it draws.

"Santiago, hold up vato, I'm here!" Javier screams. Fucking Chicano, yelling my name.

I put the truck in park and Johnny starts yelling back at Javier.

"Hey Big Mouth shut up. You want to advertise the fact we're here?"

"I'm sorry carnal, I didn't think."

I exit the truck and walk up to Javier's car window.

"You know what, why don't you just go to the police station and give them my name dumb shit. What's up with you hollering my name?"

"Take it easy man."

"Take it easy? You knew our appointment was at 2:00 and it's almost 2:30. What's going on with you carnal? Look at you man. You're drunk and stoned and you want to do business? I don't think so. Listen, we'll be coming through again tomorrow around the same time. If you're here and sober without the entire neighborhood aware of our meeting, then we can do business. You got it?"

"Who the fuck you think you are Mexican, wet back, pendejo? You can't talk to me like that," he screams while quickly jumping out of the car. He makes a move with his hand to his back as though he's going for his gun. With the swiftness and stealth of a coyote, Johnny runs up from behind him pushing his antique .38 Police Special in Javier's neck.

"¿Que haces pinche? Tranquilo y tú también Carlos no mueves. Entiendes? [What's going on. Calm down and you too Carlos don't move. Understand?]"

142

"Si mon, solo bueno, solo bueno carnal [Ya man, only good, only good]," Carlos responds in a quiet voice. He then puts his hands on the dashboard so we can watch that he doesn't make a move.

Johnny pulls Javier's Glock from his waist in back and hands it to me.

"I'll leave this in your mailbox when we leave. I don't think we'll be doing business together again. Suerte pinche."

We trot to the pickup and pull out of the driveway with Fish Eye standing there looking pissed off. Javier's wife starts screaming at him from the porch about bringing violence to his home in front of his children and neighbors. I pull up to his mailbox filled with uncollected mail. Johnny ejects the clip and the round in the chamber. He hands me the piece and I place it in the mailbox minus the clip. I step on the accelerator and we get gone.

"I guess we lost a customer. Johnny, you are truly my Colombian Guardian Angel. Gracias carnal, you reacted like a rattlesnake strike. How did you know he was going to go for his piece?"

"Really? You need to ask me why? I know when you're all full of pissed off, your mouth doesn't listen to your mind. I was sure you would say something to get Fish Face."

"Fish Eye," I corrected him.

"Okay, Fish Eye. I know you will make him angry and he will want to kill you. So, I hurry to back you up."

"Thanks carnal. I'm sorry you couldn't see his face when you stuck your gun in his neck. He was more than surprised."

Johnny smiles then patted me on my shoulder. "Hey pinche, I'm hungry. Let me buy you lunch at Crossroads. Then we'll head back to Bisbee. I'm excited to take part in this peyote ceremony tonight. This could be an epic event. That means a time that will be special and important in your life."

"Thanks for telling me what it is. Now tell me this, you not have enough epic events in your life to have to need more? I don't understand why you give the Devil more chances to take your Alma [soul]?"

We enjoyed an incredible lunch at Crossroads. It's one of my favorite Chicano restaurants in Tucson with a relaxed atmosphere, delicious entrees, and also reasonably priced. The drive back to Bisbee was uneventful. Johnny slept most of the way and the desert was a vision of magic.

Crow and Emmett were standing outside by their truck when we pulled in the driveway. We were early it was just 4:35 with twenty-five minutes to spare.

"We made it! Are you guys ready to go?"

"We weren't sure you'd make it back in time. Emmett had a vision that something bad happened in Tucson. Everything okay?"

"There was a small problem, but we got it worked out."

"Santiago, I think I will come with you but will not take peyotes. Will it be okay with you?"

"Sure carnal, I'm glad you decided to come along. It will be good to have you around."

We followed Screaming Crow and Emmett's pickup on Highway 191. Johnny was uncharacteristically quiet, without saying a word. Even my comments about his unwillingness to participate in the peyote ceremony went unchallenged.

"Rico, are you feeling alright? Is something wrong?"

"I don't know Santiago. I'm just not sure where we are going with our lifes. It has been more than ten years we've worked doing this crazy dangerous business and each day I get more nervous with paranoid feelings. I don't sleep really good any more. We are the only people we have for each other."

"That's not such a bad thing. Not many people have a friendship like ours."

"I'm not saying that it isn't good, I mean we should have more people we know around us. Instead, all we have is criminals, gang members, thieves, drug dealers, killers, and backstabbers. Most of the women we know are thieves and prostitutes. I'm just not liking being here one minute, next then over there, then back again to nowhere. Just when I catch my breath we are gone again somewhere chasing tomorrow to get ahead of yesterday. You know what I mean?"

"Sounds like a wonderful way to spend your life." I add a smile and laugh to lighten the mood. "Seriously my trusted carnal, I am surprised to hear you express such insightful thoughts. I didn't see this coming. Not to invalidate your feelings because this is a subject we need to definitely discuss. I just don't think this is the best time. Although, I want you to know I understand your concerns. Is it okay if we talk tomorrow on our way to San Diego?"

"Yes Santiago, I guess so. I just get so confused sometimes and just need to stand still for a while so I can catch up to myself."

"Gotcha jefe. Okay. I promise to make time to address your concerns and talk this over."

We reached Cochise Stronghold and pulled into an area shaded by tall oak and eucalyptus trees with a smooth mountain wall climbing into the sky as a backdrop. There were two teepees set up with six or seven Native American men standing outside in authentic deerskin dress. They all at once walked toward Emmett greeting him with hugs and strong handshakes as though they hadn't seen him in a long while. Screaming Crow stood next to Johnny and me when his mother came up and started hugging and kissing him. He didn't seem to like her attention but didn't say anything. There was a fire pit filled with a large amount of firewood and branches about four feet high with another pile of extra firewood next to it stacked tall.

Emmett introduced Johnny and I to his people. I knew there'd be no way I would remember their names. What surprised me was the names Emmett gave to me and Johnny when he introduced us. Johnny was introduced as Kanza [Man of the Wind] and I was named Pillan [God of stormy weather]. I didn't find out what it meant until I asked later. He was reluctant to divulge the meaning, thinking I might be insulted. However, the moniker actually fit me perfectly and I told him I liked it. He was happy that I was pleased.

They all sat in a circle and began cleaning the peyote buttons. I was amazed by the large amount they had. Darla, Crow's mother, along with another very attractive woman started the huge campfire. After what felt like only a few minutes the fire raged with the flames dancing high into the now almost dark sky.

There was a good-sized creek running between the tree line and the mountain wall which was now a deep crimson and rose color from the intense Arizona sunset. The water in the creek was clear and refreshingly cold. I splashed some on my face to wash off the day's stress and Johnny did the same, smiling back at me.

"This is fantastic, isn't Johnny? It's been a long time since I've felt this relaxed. Nature just has a way of getting inside of you and calming you down."

"Si, soy muy tranquilo también jefe."

We walked to the campsite and sat down around the fire. Emmett sat next me and started telling me about the legend of Cochise and the struggle against the United States Government. I felt privileged with Emmett giving such personal attention to me.

He could tell my interest was genuine. They were brewing peyote tea which was easier to ingest than eating peyote buttons. He informed me that there would be moments during the ceremony that I didn't need to participate in and to just be comfortable observing. However, if I had a vision or a paranormal experience I was to tell him immediately. Although he didn't think we would have any type of supernatural experience being we weren't Chiricahua.

Johnny retrieved our backpacks, and cooler still filled with some ice, cold juice, sodas, and water. He also grabbed a couple of large moving blankets we had in the truck. He spread them out over the coarse sand making it more comfortable. They were large enough to share with others. When the peyote tea was ready it was passed around in a large wooden bowl. Emmett added one more fact to his story. Cochise was supposedly buried somewhere here in the Stronghold although the actual location is unknown. Also, this day, June 8th was the date of his death. Johnny passed the large bowl to me after he had taken a small drink. I was going to ask how much I should drink but it somehow seemed unimportant. I took a large gulp, then quickly took another drink and passed the bowl to Emmett. He raised it to the sky and said some words I thought might be a prayer in Chiricahua.

"Rico, I thought you didn't want to do any peyote. Did you actually take a drink?"

"Yes, I did Bigotes. All of a sudden my mind changed. I don't know why, it just did."

"I'm glad you decided to come along on the adventure into the cosmic unknown."

"Okay, don't start with that mumbo jumbo shit. It makes me all scared inside."

The aftertaste of the peyote tea was bitter, coating my tongue and entire mouth with a thick texture. I looked around the fire at the other passengers on this psychedelic journey and they all seemed to be perfectly content sporting big smiles with sparkling eyes. After 45 minutes, my stomach started to rumble loudly and wasn't sure if anyone else heard it. For a short moment, I thought I was going to vomit but the urge passed without incident. My vision was starting to get a little blurry and my body felt elastic. I noticed seeing in the flames of the fire different images. There were faces of no one in particular, just faces. Then flowers appeared with scenes of trees swaying and their leaves dancing to a distant melody I heard playing somewhere in the distance. The others had all put on decorative headbands staring into the fire with intense expressions. Emmett began shaking a maraca as the others started humming a melody with someone playing a drum. The sound resonated throughout the night with a distinct echo. Johnny sat with his eyes closed rocking to the rhythm of the drum. I looked up into the night sky and watched the flames touching the darkness.

Then I had an intense feeling as if someone was standing behind me. It made me terribly uncomfortable; I didn't want to turn around to take a look. Then I felt a hand on my left shoulder. Quickly I checked if it might have been Emmett sitting beside me, but he wasn't there. When I looked to see if it might have been Johnny on the other side he was gone as well. In fact, I couldn't see anyone else around the fire. I was alone, all by myself. Everyone else had vanished. They had all simply disappeared. I worked up the courage to turn around to see who was standing behind me. What I saw surprised me but for some reason I didn't feel any fear at all. In front of me stood a Native American with a long white headdress with feathers trailing down to his ankles. He smiled at me with glowing amber eyes. Softly he spoke to me in his native language which I didn't speak, but I understood what he said as though he communicated to me telepathically.

After telling me his message the vision slowly faded with him still smiling as he disappeared into the dark. I'm unable to remember what he told me but I felt a strong surge of energy flowing through my body touching me deep down to my soul.

I turned back to face the fire and amazingly everyone had returned. Then, during a heavy psychedelic rush I noticed I had become surrounded by Colorado River Toads. There looked to be twenty-five, maybe thirty, toads staring directly at me, not moving at all. I became somewhat unsettled by the amphibians congregating around me. Emmett was sitting next to me once again. I got his attention by pulling at his sleeve and asked him if he could see the toads as well. He smiled and started patting me on the back. Then he began dancing and chanting as though he was celebrating. He announced to the others that a miracle had taken place. Everyone came over to see the toads that had gathered around me. They all began dancing and chanting with some reaching out to touch me. Some of them rubbed the hair on my head.

Emmett explained I was being visited by my animal guide but never had he seen this kind of response. There were so many toads appearing it was truly a magical phenomena.

Johnny jumped up and moved away from the group. "Santiago, can you not see all the toads around you! What is going on?" He hollered.

"Relax amigomio, they just stopped by to pay their respects. They won't hurt you."

He isn't comforted by my explanation and takes refuge inside the truck.

Emmett, still dancing, comes over to me, careful not to step on my amphibian admirers.

"The toad is a good omen as your spirit guide. You are someone full of strong magic as strong as that of a brujo. The toad is a symbol of wisdom and intelligence. Also, you will have good luck in your life and be protected from evil. You have a need to wander from place to place. Never staying somewhere for a long time."

"Emmett, I need to tell you about an incredible vision I had before the toads appeared."

"It is very strange that you have a vision and you discover your spirit guide without having any Native American blood. Tell me about your vision."

I explained to him what had manifested behind me touching my shoulder. The vision with glowing amber eyes, long white headdress, and how he communicated to me telepathically. I also mentioned how everyone had disappeared leaving me alone. He asked what he told me, looking disappointed when I reported that I didn't remember what it was he said.

Fatigue had set in and the effect of the peyote was wearing off. I walked to the truck noticing Johnny asleep laying on the back seat. I took a look at the clock on the dash saying it was 1:30 in the morning. It could have only been around 6:30, maybe 7:00 when I did the peyote. Where have I been for seven hours? This loss of time is something I seem to experience whenever I do psychedelics. I haven't been able to explain the phenomenon even after experiencing it many times.

"Santi, you are very fortunate at this ceremony," Screaming Crow says walking over to me. "Emmett wants you to become a member of the Chiricahua People. He says you are good luck for them."

"I'm not able to deal with that right now. I'll explain to Emmett."

"You should know that you are now seen as someone with powerful magic and a window to see into the spirit world."

"Ya wanna know what I am? I'm just a kid from the southside of Chicago who attracted some toads and had a hallucination of some spirit during a peyote trip. I'm nothing special and don't have any superpowers. So don't go blowing this thing out of proportion."

"Some people are jealous of you having a vision and discovering your spirit totem all in one ceremony. There are some that have never had a vision in their entire lifetime."

"They'll just have to deal with it."

I returned to the campfire and sat down next to Emmett. All the toads had gone except one extremely huge toad. It moved closer to me then started croaking over and over in rapid succession. I noticed everyone was staring at me causing me to feel self-conscious.

"Hey, Emmett do you ever experience losing time during a peyote ritual? I don't understand how or why it happens to me every time."

"Time moves faster the farther you are away from earth or gravity. The fact it appears you lose time is because during a peyote experience you leave this reality and are in a different dimension. When you return it looks like you have lost time. That is the best I can explain it. Hope that helps."

"Yes, it does. Thanks."

"When you remember what the spirit said to you, please find a way to tell me. Okay?"

"I will for sure, I promise. I think I'm going to lay down. I've had quite a night. Thanks for this, Emmett."

"It was my pleasure, Santiago. Good night."

Years later I was in a coma for thirty-five days caused by a sepsis infection. When I recovered and woke up, I brought back with me a strange memory. I remembered what it was the vision had told me on that night in Cochise Stronghold.

No Boats

"Santiago, what are you doing to yourself? Why you sticking your arm with a needle? Stop! Stop now! You are really scaring me," Johnny yells, startling me with his surprise entrance.

How did he get in? Did he just walk in? I didn't lock the door? Damnit, what's wrong with you Santiago?

Johnny continues with his rant. "Listen to me you stupid gringo. I mean it! If I must have to hit you on the head with this hammer, I will!" He threatens me holding a hammer above his head, acting as if he's ready to strike a blow.

I finish shooting up and pull the syringe out of my arm. The Speedball [a combination of heroin and cocaine] delivers a righteous high with an intense rush. I'm on the verge of passing out and vomiting as well. One thing for certain, I'm unable to respond to Rico's demands while the drugs fight it out for control of my body. I can hear Johnny's voice, although it sounds faint, far off in the distance even though he's standing only two feet in front of me. The only thing it seems I'm able to focus on is wondering where in the hell did Johnny find that hammer? There's a break between the drug's fight to control me. I find the strength to respond to Johnny's interrogation.

"I know you're upset with me right now, but I'm too high to carry on a coherent conversation. But I'd like to know where in the hell did you find the hammer?" An intense rush from the cocaine causes me to jump up and I start pacing quickly around the room.

Johnny grabs my arm and pulls me to a stop, he then splashes water on it and starts wiping off the blood with the bottom part of his shirt.

"You're a fucked up mess. Look at you! Look!" He screams, pointing at my reflection in the mirror on the living room wall. I greet my reflection with a stupid grin which makes him angry.

"Santiago, I never have want to so much punch you in your face as I do now!"

"Hey, Johnny, can you just leave me the fuck alone right now? I'm not in the mood to deal with you. You're harshing my high," I slur.

"Here, I got something to harsh you being high, cabron." Then, for the first time in all the years we've known one another, he hauls off and punches me in the face. The blow lands with the force of a heavyweight boxer's left hook and I wake up on the floor. There's blood running from my nose which I'm sure is broken again for the thousandth time. Johnny is sitting on the sofa talking to himself in Spanish and the conversation isn't cordial.

"What the fuck, shithead? What do you think you're doing? I know I've probably deserved that for years but you sucker punched me when I'm high? That hardly seems cool."

"You know I love you, Santi. It hurt me so much to see you do that to yourself. I don't want you to die. Then I have no one in the whole world to count on, to look out for me, to make me laugh so much, to teach me smart things, or to be always around for me," he says sincerely while smashing the syringe into the tabletop.

"Well first, I think you need to work on your 'Tough Love' therapy. Secondly, how the hell does my getting high become all about you? There's times I don't want to live anymore but it doesn't mean I want to die. It's not an attempt to kill myself I'm too much of a coward to take my own life."

I can feel my nose still trickling blood and Johnny throws a box of tissues at me which I don't catch and it hits me in the face.

"Where did you learn to throw a punch like that?" I mention while I attempt to get up from the floor. I'm unsuccessful for a third time as my hands slip on the tile and I fall back down slamming my head against a table leg in the process. Once again, I become unconscious.

Slowly, I come to life noticing the darkness has replaced the daylight. I'm lying on the sofa, pillow under my head, my mother's knitted afghan covering me and a damp washcloth over my nose. There's voices and laughter echoing from the kitchen, but I'm unconcerned with who Johnny is entertaining. He took care of me after I was incapacitated, plus I've never had to worry about my welfare when Johnny was on watch. Even Jesus Christ wouldn't be able to get to me if he was standing guard.

I hear people coming into the living room. I'm not sure why but I close my eyes pretending to be asleep. I instantly recognize one voice talking with J.R.

"How long has he been out? Maybe you should wake him up and check if he's okay."

It's Ishmael from Sinaloa, Mexico who is arriving here on Saturday. Then a shock of uncertainty runs through my body. It's Thursday, isn't it? Still Thursday, I haven't been unconscious for two days? I decide to end my ploy of being asleep, waking up, and acting surprised to see Ishmael.

"Hey Patrón [Boss] surprised to see you. When did you get in?"

I was hoping my assumption of it being Thursday was correct. I didn't want to appear unreliable not knowing what day it was. He is a high-ranking officer in the cartel and personal friend of 'El Jefe' [the Chief].

I inspected the coffee table where I had shot up and it was clean without any evidence of my actions. Johnny has proved himself to be a reliable friend looking out for my well-being.

"Yes, I know I'm here two days early, thought it was a good idea in case I encountered any problems. I had to be driven to Guatemala from Mazatlan and take a plane from there because it is getting too difficult to be in public. The Federales are really putting on the pressure."

Oh, Santiago, you lucky bastard, you finally get a break from the guardians of the cosmos.

"Besides, it will give us some time to enjoy each other's company," he says as he walks toward me. I stand and he gives me a hug.

"So good to see you, Santiago," he whispered.

Ishmael's top soldier and bodyguard enters from the kitchen and begins pulling me away from Ishmael, thinking I may be attacking him.

"No Lobo [Wolf], it's alright, it's alright just a friendly hug," Ishmael says calling off his 'Wolf'.

I've known Lobo since we were kids, he lived in the pueblo where my mother grew up. We met there when visiting my mother's family in Mexico. He never seemed to be very bright, I always thought he may have been borderline retarded. One thing for sure, he enjoyed handing out pain. He wasn't a bully, but if you crossed him or humiliated him, you could bet there was a beatdown coming; he had a very short fuse. I always brought him a baseball cap when we visited. He seemed genuinely excited with the cap and appreciated my gift. Years later, my generosity proved to be a valuable courtesy. I gained his respect and along with it came his unwavering protection.

"Hey Lobo, I wondered if you were coming with Ishmael. You remember me, don't you?"

"Yes, I remember who you are. Where's my ballcap? Do you have one for me?" He asks with a serious expression.

"You do remember! No, I don't have one for you but I'll tell you what. We should have lunch together and after that we'll go shopping for a ball cap, maybe a jersey as well. Sound good, Lobo?"

"Are we going to lunch with him tomorrow, Patron?" He asks Ishmael.

"That would be great. We'll meet you here at about 1:00. Okay with you, Santiago?"

"Just fine. I'm going to need to have Johnny with me, if that's alright. He's my partner and should hear all the details about the run firsthand."

"Of course, bring your partner, he's quite the comedian. I've got an appointment with an associate right now, so we'll be leaving. We'll get together tomorrow for sure. I just wanted to stop by and say hello. I thought it was a good idea to let you know we were here early. Oh, something I need to ask, why are your eyes all black and blue? You look like you were kicked by a mule."

"I'll fill you in at lunch tomorrow, it's a long story," I tell him while walking the two of them out.

"I hope she had a good excuse for kicking your ass."

"Funny guy."

"One more thing, I gave your compadre the name of the hotel we're staying at. You have the number to my satellite phone, don't you?"

"Si patrón, yo lo tengo. Entonces mañana nos vemos."

We shake hands, I close the door, and lock it this time. I take a deep breath and walk over to the mirror in the living room to take a look at my face.

"Jesus Christ, Rico, my eyes are a deep black and blue. You really clocked me Johnniehole. It's a good thing I was high when you punched me, otherwise it might have been painful."

"You know I am very sorry for what I do. Will you forgive me forever?"

"I'll have to think about it Rico. Thanks for covering for me with Ishmael. Cleaning up the dope and shit. You should've woken me up when he arrived. You just let people you don't know in my apartment? You didn't know who he was."

"Yes, I know him. I met him when we were in Mexico at your cousin's Rancho. When he told me who he was and his name I know it was okay."

"Guess I should've learned by now to trust your judgment."

"Santiago, why you have not told me about having a run? Don't you think it's something you should tell me? And I should have the choice to say yes or no."

"I wasn't sure it was going to happen, so I didn't want to say anything."

"You say last time you are done with this work. You're too old to go back to prison. So, tell me what are you doing?"

"If you're not interested in partnering up, I'll get somebody else to work with. Although you should know the pay for this donkey haul is a king's fortune. I figured this would be our final smuggling operation. We can walk away from this hazardous employment with more than enough to retire on," I announced with a smile.

"You say for five years you are too old and each is the last time you quit. But you are a liar to yourself. Always saying, "You are back in the saddle again, giddyup.""

"Let me tell you what information I have been told so far. We'll take a boat from ..."

Johnny interrupts. "No boats! I tell you last time no boats. But we had to go in a boat and it sinked when the Puerto Rican guy Rodolfo crash us into a big ship. Then for almost a whole day we were in the ocean before the pescadores rescue us. I tell you many times I'm afraid of the deep ocean and you know I can't swim. No boat, I'm out!" He stands and walks into the kitchen saying, "no boat" over and over again.

Four years ago, me and Johnny along with this Puerto Rican shit for brains were taking a load from Cartagena to Grand Bahama. He was acting as our captain and navigator and was recommended by El Jefe. He was an experienced sailor having made this trek many times before. It was a new moon night, dark with a calm sea as we entered the windward strait between Cuba and Haiti. Johnny and I had both fallen asleep knowing our experienced captain had everything under control.

We woke up to the sound of our boat being crushed by a large cargo ship that had run into us. Our experienced captain had also fallen asleep running us straight into the path of the monster ship.

Instantly we sank, after being completely destroyed. The ship most likely had no idea it had run into us and just kept on going. I found a lifejacket, immediately giving it to Johnny knowing he couldn't swim. I didn't see the captain anywhere among the debris. I called for him over again but never received a reply. If he was dead it saved me from having to kill the Son of a Bitch.

I found Johnny floating along bobbing up and down to the gentle motion of the waves. I pushed part of a broken wooden door toward him and hung onto it next to him.

The following late afternoon we were spotted by a Dominican fishing trawler and rescued, and that is the reason for Johnny's refrain of, "No boats! No boats!"

"Fine you pussy! Then I'll call Javier and see if he might be interested. You've gone and made your decision without knowing anything about the run. And now the rules are I'm not able to tell you anything more."

"You know I have afraid of the water and especially El Mar. But you no care for my feelings. You just think I am going to do what you say or want me to do."

"Can I explain to you the few facts I've been made aware of concerning the run? After I was told, I took your fear of the ocean into consideration when I was first informed about the boat. Listen Johnny, this is a forty-two foot cabin cruiser, small yacht. It's bigger than the boat we took from Cartagena to Isla Mujeres and you weren't scared then."

"I was horrible scared. I just didn't want you to know because you'd start making jokes about me"

"I'm not that kinda guy."

"You for sure are going to Hell because you lie so much."

160

"Listen, that boat was just a twenty-four-footer, seven and a half meters or so. The boat we're taking is twice as big. It's a forty-eight foot, fourteen and a half meters, small yacht. Here let me pull up a picture from the internet."

After inspecting the photo of the forty-eight-foot cabin cruiser he commented on how luxurious it was but he wasn't sold on the idea.

"You know who's boat it is?"

"Ya, I know who's boat it *was*, but I don't think he's in any condition to object if we pirate it. Now I don't know the destination or the weight of the load. We'll get that information from Ishmael at the meeting tomorrow. So, I need to know if you're in or out, Rico."

He was actually taking his time thinking over his decision. It was kind of pissing me off. After all the insane life-threatening expeditions I willingly went on with him, never having a second thought as to my participation, here he was thinking twice about taking part in this run.

"You're not considering turning down this once in a lifetime opportunity, are you? And besides, how could you even consider not partnering up in the last smuggling operation of Los Dos Chiflados?"

"Now you are a big liar. I don't think you will ever stop this kind of work. You like to take the risk and the danger. You get some kind of high feeling from doing it. I can see it in your eyes. You will be an old man sixty years and still running loads, if you live that long."

"Hey Johnny, don't get so serious on me. Tell me when did you get your Doctor of Psychology Medical License? Now stop with this crazy talk, let's hop in our saddles and giddyup."

"See, there you start with the giddyup. You remember when we were in Arizona at the peyotes ceremony?"

"Of course, what are you trying to say carnal? Come on, cut to the chase."

"I try to tell you when driving back from Tucson in the truck. But you said we would talk about the sadness in my heart later but we never talked about it again, ever. I want to try telling you so many times but never is the right time you always say."

Johnny takes a deep breath and with a long sigh, his lips begin quivering and he starts crying. He's balling like a kid who lost his dog. I put my hand on his shoulder and squeezed, attempting to comfort him, but he pushes it away. He walks out on the balcony staring out into the darkness. I can still hear him sobbing loudly, he's hyperventilating, unable to catch his breath.

"Don't jump, Johnny!" I holler jokingly.

"I won't jump. See you start making jokes."

I walk out onto the balcony standing next to him. "Hey amigo mio que haces? [Friend of mine, what are you doing?] What's with the brush off when I put my hand on your shoulder?"

"Santiago, in all the time we know each other and are best friends, there are sometimes when I don't like you so much. But that feeling always goes away fast because I know no one in the world is a better friend than you."

"Yes, I'll agree with that statement. I know there's something more. Come on spit it out. What do you want to say?"

"I want to have a different life. Not have to always look over my shoulder, watch my back. I would like to have a house that is mine instead of always moving from apartment to apartment. We never live in a place for more than a few months. I think maybe it might be good to have a girlfriend or maybe even a wife. Never am I with someone for longer than eight or nine months. I think I am done with this life of beating the Devil. Maybe I will get a real job and go to work everyday at a Walmart or the Home Depot. Do you understand? I wanted to tell you for a long time but was afraid it would make you sad or you get mad at me. I have felt this way since after my mother died and I wasn't there for her funeral."

"I had no clue you were feeling this way, Johnny. I've always thought you enjoyed our lifestyle. There is no one better at what we do than you. I can always count on you to get the job done. If you want to quit, then quit, it's good to know when to stop. Do you have any money saved?"

"Yes, enough to get by on for a year or so. You are not mad at me?"

"No, not mad, just downhearted that our business relationship has come to an end. But I want to know you will always be considered the best friend anyone could ever hope for. I have been a fortunate man to have had you in my life."

"I'm sorry, Santiago. It has to be this way. Do you understand?"

"I'm trying to understand. I'll tell you what, let's go out and tear up this town. As you say, 'Get drunker than a hundred indians.' What do you say vato? I'll even let you buy."

That drunken night was the last time I saw my trusted friend. We promised to keep in touch, but you know how that goes. I made the run with a Venezuelan guy I knew for quite awhile. The trip was a success. But Johnny was right about one thing. I couldn't stop taking part in this type of business. There would be many more last times.

Where in the World is Johnny Rico

I'd been living in Costa Rica, bored with the passive lifestyle I adopted in my retirement. I thought a remedy to my melancholy might be a short vacation away from this paradise. In any case, there had been too many rises and falls of the tides since I had last buried my toes in the sand of a Colombian beach.

Cartagena was beckoning me to become a willing hostage of her casual elegance, comforting charms, and the soothing touch of her ocean breeze. It had been close to eight years since I'd last seen her, back when I'd finally bid farewell to the "business", and to my friend and former running partner, Johnny Rico, as well.

Upon my arrival, I hailed a taxi for the short ride to Hotel Caribe, an elegant five-star inn with a friendly, accommodating staff, nestled on the Boca Grande peninsula. Before I knew it, I was comfortably settled into my suite with a millionaire's vista of the city.

Back in the bold reckless days of my youth, I'd be wired, revved up, and ready to take on the night. But, owing to my advancing age, I'd decided to relax in my room for the evening instead. It was close to 7:30 on a Saturday night, with nothing much on the agenda.

I enjoyed an almost-hot shower and ordered room service, which was delivered much more quickly than expected. I focused my attention on the television, hoping to find something I could fall asleep to.

As I flipped through channel after channel, I was excited to discover several adult options. My excitement quickly dwindled, however, after thinking I might be charged a ridiculous fee for this service. Checking my hotel receipt for a possible clue produced no information and referencing the brochures in the room ended with the same result.

Heading downstairs, I took a seat at the bar. I order a Scotch, neat, which the bartender pours with a generous hand.

"Thanks, carnal," I say. "Appreciate your generosity. Kind of dead in here tonight, wouldn't ya say?"

"Usually like this, early in the evening," he replies. "Are you staying at the hotel?"

"Yes, I am. Tell me, how long have you been working here?"

"I think almost five years now. I like it very much. The people are very nice and always have interesting stories."

"Bet you meet many new faces," I tell him. "Let me ask you a question. I noticed on my television I have access to all channels, including certain pay channels. Do you know if this is included with the cost of my room?"

"If you have a suite on the top floor, I believe they are all free. Also, spa with massage and breakfast is included. Would you like me to ask the front desk to make sure?"

"Thank you, but that won't be necessary. Say, what's your name, so I won't have to call you bartender?"

"Sergio, but everyone just calls me Serg. What is your name?"

"Santiago, but you can call me Santi, or Bigotes, if you'd like."

"Bigotes, I like it. I could tell you were Mexican because of your Spanish, but you look very Italian as well."

"I'm from all over. I live in Costa Rica now, but I have spent much time in Mexico. I lived here in Cartagena for quite some time as well, back eight years ago, right here in Barrio San Diego."

"Bigotes, you have a face that is familiar to me. Where did you hangout, back when you lived here?"

"Everywhere and anywhere there were women, wine, and song. My friend and I had a favorite spot, right near my old apartment: Tu Candela Bar. Looking forward to going back there, maybe tomorrow."

"Before I came here, that is where I worked, only as a waiter not bartender."

"Really?"

"Yes. I remember you, Bigotes, always with another guy who laughed real loud. Rico was his name, I think. You both holler at each other and fight all the time. I remember you were the thinner one, and your hair was much shorter."

"Well spank me with a spatula, that's incredible. Johnny Rico, that's him! You have a strong memory, my friend. Those days were quite some time ago."

"You came to Cartagena to see your old friend again?"

"No, I haven't been able to find him in years. I'm just on a mini-vacation, a short change of scenery is all. You have a great evening, Serg. I'm going to head back up to my room now. I appreciate your help."

"No problema. I'll be here until around 10:00. There is a wedding reception, here at the hotel tonight. Glad I'm not working the bar! See you around, Bigotes."

"Nos vemos, Serg."

Suddenly, my room somehow didn't seem to fit the size of my temperament anymore. There wasn't a movie on that interested me, and even the adult channels failed to capture my attention, despite them being free.

Damn, Serg had remembered Rico and me after all this time. I'd tried to get in touch with J.R. on several occasions in the past, but without success. His mother had long since died, and his sister didn't want anything to do with him anymore, leaving me with nothing but a string of old memories and disconnected phone numbers. But that's life.

Putting these thoughts aside, I make the decision to head out into the night, hoping to revisit some old familiar haunts. Mothers hide your daughters, Santiago is on the prowl!

I hail a taxi, and within minutes I'm back in Old Cartagena. The city's quaint charm sparkles in the salty evening air.

After accomplishing my 4 D's for the evening (dinner, drugs, drinking, and dancing), the mission bell rings once, signaling 1am. I chase down another taxi for the short drive back to the hotel, only this time with my companion, Valeria, now in tow. We had met earlier in the night, enjoying each other's company at Cafe Havana, where a ten-piece salsa band had been playing.

My girlfriend de jour is an absolute vision of loveliness: humorous, compassionate, reasonably priced, and a talented dancer to boot. We were both pleasantly high from all the booze and cocaine chasers. By all appearances, she appeared ready to wrestle with the anaconda.

We arrive at the hotel, deciding first to enjoy a cocktail at the bar. Surprisingly, the room had filled with a large crowd while I'd been out, everyone dancing to a DJ spinning reggaeton, my newly adopted favorite genre of music.

We were fortunate to find two seats at the bar. It was then I recalled Sergio mentioning a wedding reception at the hotel that night. Generally, I make it a rule to not attend weddings, because I always feel so helpless to stop the proceedings. As I always say, marriage is what happens when dating goes too far!

I ordered our drinks, and Valeria headed off to the ladies room to do a bump. When she returned, I excused myself to use the restroom as well, peeking into the adjacent banquet hall as I walked past. There I observed a fair-sized group, dancing in celebration of the two willing victims of love.

That's when it suddenly hits me.

Above the noise of the reception, my ears perk up to the sound of that old, familiar laugh. It rings out in my heart like a song from long ago.

Could it really be? The lunatic laughter of the only man I've ever called a friend?

Stopping for a closer look, I peruse the guests inside. And sure enough, seated at none other than the bridal table, is the man I suspect to be "His Riconess" himself.

He was grossly overweight with long, stringy hair and a short, scruffy beard. He wore an all-white suit with dark sunglasses, despite us being indoors at night. His overall look was one I'd call "Neo-Italian." I watch him as he takes a long drink of wine, then erupts into another one of his crazed cackles.

There can be no mistaking it. After years of searching in vain, I have finally stumbled upon the one and only, Johnny Rico.

I watched as the large, unattractive bride sat down beside him, kissing his stubbly, blubbery lips as the guests all applauded, clinking their glasses with flatware. It must have been a cold winter in Hell, if a storm of this magnitude had breached the Devil's compound.

Rico got hitched. He was now a married man. I should really congratulate this hostage of love, I thought, then pay my condolences to the wide bride on her fine choice of a husband.

I returned to the bar, where seated on my stool was some scoundrel trying to woo Valeria away from me. He makes a hasty exit as I walk up, planting a kiss on my rent-a-date for the evening.

"Don't go anywhere," I tell her. "I'll be right back."

Flagging down one of the waiters, I asked if I could borrow his blazer, tipping him generously for the rental. Next, I draped a white towel over my arm, donning my reading glasses for effect. My look now complete, I set out on my ambush, returning to the banquet hall as a hotel employee.

Walking briskly past the bridal table, I came around the back of it, completely unnoticed by my old friend. Standing behind him, I slowly leaned forward, whispering just loud enough for others to hear.

"Excuse me sir, but you appear to be very drunk. We won't be allowed to serve you any more alcohol this evening. In addition, your guests have purchased drinks from the bar, with a bill almost four hundred dollars. We will need you to pay it immediately!"

He begins to stand, but I force him back down, pushing down hard on his shoulders. He whips back around at me, ready to strike, but that's when he sees my face.

In an instant, his expression of rage dissolves into joyous disbelief.

"Un milagro! Milagro a Dios! Carnal eres tu? [A miracle! Miracle my God. My buddy, is it you?]"

Leaping to his feet, he wraps his arms around me, squeezing all the air from my lungs.

"Someone told me you were dead," he said, as I'm attempting to extricate myself from his grasp. "Killed in Mexico, they said, by enemies of your cousin."

"I was killed," I replied, "but they made one mistake – they didn't kill me twice!"

"I am so happy to see you alive, carnal."

Meanwhile, Valeria is now standing near the entrance of the banquet hall. I signal for her to come and join us. She smiles and walks over, every man in the room fixated on her beauty as she graciously glides across it.

I order a bottle of mescal for the table to help get this party started.

"Thank you, Santi!" Johnny screams. "Now we get drunker than a hundred indians!"

Half a bottle and several lines of coke later, we were both up onstage, singing together our karaoke favorite: *With a Little Help From My Friends*.

We finish our little number and Johnny immediately starts taking off his clothes, asking the crowd if they want to see an obre de arte [work of art]. He whips out his dick and starts prancing around the hall like a ballerina, causing quite an uproar in the process.

His bride doesn't seem to find his little performance quite so funny, however. Her attempts to intervene are met with an inebriated Johnny completely ignoring her pleas for him to stop.

It was then that I asked the DJ to play *Satisfaction*, by the Stones. I sing and dance in my best Mick Jagger impression, my spastic moves sending Johnny into hysterics along with the rest of the crowd.

Finally, we settled back down around our table, slamming more mescal as Johnny apologized to his bride and their guests for his antics. Meanwhile, our fans had raised their applause once more, clapping and demanding an encore.

Retaking the stage, we then sang our other song, *I Shot the Sheriff* (Marley version), only changing the lyrics to where we shot both the sheriff and the deputy.

During the lead break, Johnny pulls out the same .38 he's had since I'd first met him, firing off rounds into the ceiling like a drunk cowboy in a saloon. In response, the wedding guests hit the floor, some taking refuge under tables, others fleeing screaming for the exits.

Now, I know my reaction should have been to disarm my lunatic sidekick immediately. However, I'd found myself in such a state of disbelief, all I could do was laugh, completely unafraid of the danger.

Within minutes, two security guards storm the banquet hall, demanding that Johnny surrender his pistol immediately. Knowing him, I knew their request would be met with defiance.

As they reached the stage, Johnny tossed the pistol over to me, thus diverting their attention. As they passed him by, he swept up a nearby chair and slammed it into the back of one of them. Meanwhile, I pointed the gun at the other, ordering him to stop.

I added that I would blow his fucking balls off if he didn't.

Side note: Threatening a Columbian with death is not always a successful deterrent, but living without their dick or balls is a fate they consider worse than death.

He stops as ordered, standing motionless with is hands out before him. He tries appealing to my sensibility, which has been all but drowned in tequila by this point. Acting on the tequila's advice instead, I kick him straight in the balls, connecting with the force of a punter. He drops to his knees like a nun at mass, grabbing his crotch in pain.

Meanwhile, Johnny is punching the shit out of the other guard on the floor, his porky wife literally on his back, screaming for him to stop. She obviously has no idea of the man she's just married.

And here I am, standing over my own victim, still pointing the gun at this terrified man.

"Bigotes todo bien carnal? No el mata! No el mata! [Mister Mustache, everything good? Don't kill him! Don't kill him!]," Johnny yells.

"Why not?" I yell back. "He tried to hurt you, mi hermano. I can't let that type of behavior go unpunished."

The guy starts crying, begging for his life. I tell him I don't understand Spanish, and with his life on the line, he chooses to argue that he heard me speaking Spanish earlier, accusing me of lying with a gun pointed at his head. I am so overwhelmed by his stupidity to argue with a crazed gunman, I burst into another uncontrollable laughing jag. My buddy joins in, his wife still riding him like a bucking bronco.

Meanwhile, some of the guests have returned, watching the situation intently. The DJ, for his part, seems totally unfazed by the fiasco. He puts on *Street Fighting Man* by the Stones, and I resume my Jagger dance over the security guard on the floor. Everyone begins laughing and applauding once more.

Eventually, I extend my hand to help the security guard to his feet, which he accepts.

What he didn't know was that I'd folded two hundred-dollar bills into my palm. He inspects them surreptitiously, then walks over to his partner, passing him one in like manner. Suddenly, they are both grinning like game show winners.

Our celebration is cut short, however, by the arrival of six or seven Colombian police officers with rifles, some of them adorned with helmets and shields. Valeria comes up from behind and slowly takes the pistol from my hand, pulls up her skirt, and tucks it away in her panties. She whispers that I can retrieve it later, kissing me on the cheek.

The cops scream at the DJ to turn off the music, pushing through the crowd without apology.

They immediately confront the security guards, demanding an explanation.

"Lo que está pasando aquí y solo tener un informe de que alguien está disparando un arma a la gente. Diga me! [What's going on here? We had a call that someone was firing a gun shooting at people. Tell me!]," a large military type demands to know.

"This is my wedding party," Johnny interjects, "and the only guns here are those you brought yourself!"

"Hey Johnny," I tell him, "how about you let the guards answer and shut the fuck up? Use those lips to kiss that new wife of yours, instead of inciting these officers just doing their jobs."

"We thought there was a problem when we heard screaming and came to investigate," one of the security guards informs the police officers. "It was this one," he says, pointing at Johnny. "He was acting all crazy with his Mexican buddy over there, pretending to shoot each other."

"The song had gunshots in it," the DJ explains. "Everything is good. Solo bueno, solo bueno."

He puts on some narco-corrido song, *Sangunarios del M1* [Bloodthirsty Men of the M1], demonstrating the realism of the gunshots.

The cops appear unconvinced, however, ordering Johnny and I to stand against the wall. They start frisking me, asking us both over and over where the gun is stashed. Some of the other guests continue to explain to the officers there was no gun.

"Where is the gun, Bigotes?" Johnny starts joking. "Just give them the fucking gun so they'll leave us alone!"

"Are you for real, bufo?" I scream at the bastard. "What the fuck is wrong with you? Are you fucking insane?"

"This is my wedding reception," he sneers at the cops, "and I would appreciate it if you officers either left or joined the party!"

"I see you found your friend!" a voice rings out from behind us. We both turn to see Sergio approach. "There you both are, arguing and yelling the same as I remember in the past ..."

"Officers," he continues, "I know both these gentlemen very well. What you're accusing them of is not at all what happened here."

"Who are you?" a cop barks at him. "Do you work here?"

"I am Sergio Mendez Ortiz, the Bar and Banquet Manager," he answers. "I appreciate your quick response to what you thought was a dangerous situation, but whoever reported the incident was incorrect."

"And how do you know that? Did you witness the event?"

"I did," Sergio tells them, "and I can assure you there was no gun."

Eventually, by some miracle, the cops begrudgingly accept Sergio's explanation. As they start heading for the exit, that's when Johnny decides to open his big mouth again, spewing out comment after comment of contempt.

"You should apologize for ruining my wedding party!" he calls out after them. "Aren't you even going to say sorry? You disrespected my wife, my friend, and all our guests."

The commander turns to Johnny with a none-to-pleased look on his face.

"One more word out of you," he warns, "and your bride will be sleeping alone tonight, while you become a bride to some convict. Understand?"

I run the short distance over to my carnal, literally clamping my hand over his mouth. He tries to spit out another smart-ass comment regardless, prying at my hand in an attempt to incarcerate himself.

"He understands, officer," I assure him. "Thank you for your ..."

The DJ cranks the music back up to a deafening volume, and suddenly everyone is dancing once again.

I walk over to Sergio and shake his hand, passing my remaining money to him.

"Sergio, we appreciate you rescuing us from being arrested."

"No problema," he says with a wink. "Just don't let me see that gun around here again."

"What gun?" Johnny asks, laughing.

It is then he gets his first taste of married life with a pissed-off Latina. Without missing a beat, his bride starts in on him in front of the assembled guests.

Completely ignoring her, Johnny turns to me instead, drawing me into a tight embrace. He still can't stop laughing, tears running down his face.

"I've missed you carnal," he says sadly. "You are more than family to me."

"I know, Johnny," I tell him. "Let me toast to your wedding. Do you have any money on you? Lend me a bill 'til I can get to a machine. I gave everything I had to the security guards and Sergio, and I want to tip the DJ for giving us an alibi as well."

"No money?" he asks, his bride still yelling in his ear. "You aren't even going to give us a wedding gift?"

"Wedding gift?" I cry in indignation. "I just spent three hundred dollars paying off people for your stupid antics! Wedding gift? I sincerely hope your screaming wife has the patience to put up with your mental illness."

Finally, she gives up on her rant, exhausted by his utter lack of recognition. She quickly walks away with an older woman I assume to be her mother.

"Johnny, I think she is crying," I tell him. "Go and apologize and tell her this type of behavior is likely to continue over the course of your marriage."

He stumbles off after her, and I go to find an ATM.

I find Valeria waiting for me at a table, being hit on by every guy at the party. When she notices me walking toward her, she stands and extends her hand for me to take.

Walking arm in arm, she accompanies me to an ATM down the street. Along the way, she slips her hand into my jacket pocket, depositing the gun within.

"Santi," she says, "I am ready for sex with you. Do you want to go to your room soon? You already paid for everything, and I need to call my mother to tell her I'm okay. Should I tell her I will be home Monday? I like you very much, Santi, and want to spend some time with you ..."

Now, this isn't my first initiation with a prostitute. I'd learned long ago just to fuck 'em, not fall in love with them. But Valeria is young and still hasn't learned.

Finally, we reach the ATM, withdrawing four hundred dollars in twenty-dollar bills. Meanwhile, it is 3am in a Colombian city, and I know better than to just stand there flashing my cash. After being victimized, gringos have no idea why they'd been robbed. Why? Because you deserved it for being fucking stupid, that's why.

We begin to walk back the short distance to the hotel. You can smell the aroma of bread and donuts baking from the shops nearby.

It is then that a homeless street junkie confronts us, large rock in one hand and what appears to be a steel bar of some type, maybe a curtain rod, in the other. He demands that I turn over my money, my watch, and the gold ring on my left pinky finger, which belonged to my daughter.

I first attempt to reason with him, offering a small donation to his drug fund instead. The suggestion is received poorly, and he displays his anger by swirling the curtain rod like a lightsaber, as though he were a Jedi master.

"Santi, give him the money!" Valeria says, clinging close. "I am afraid Santi, please! Tranquillo, senor, I will get it ..."

"I'm not giving this carapecha [dickface] a fucking peso!" I scream.

Next thing I know, Valeria has Johnny's gun back in her hands, pointing it directly at Skywalker.

"First of all," she says to him, "you didn't say please. Now I'm going to shoot your fucking balls off, you hijo de perra!"

At this, I instantly got a monstrous erection. What a woman! This demonstration of foreplay on her part had aroused me to a point of near ejaculation.

The wannabe Jedi scurries off, and Valeria returns the gun to my pocket once again, giggling as she softly puts a finger to her lips.

"Valeria, that was awesome, baby. Damn, you really are the total package! We have got to get back to my room ..."

She grabs me by the head, pulling me in for a kiss.

"No! No!" I protest. "Don't touch me! I'm so excited right now, I might just cum right here!"

She laughs and grabs my crotch anyway, giving it a loving squeeze.

We return to the hotel, and I immediately start pulling her toward the elevators.

"Bigotes! Bigotes!" Sergio calls from across the lobby. "Wait, I have a message for you, from your friend. He'd asked for your room number, but it is not our hotel's policy to give out personal information."

"A wonderful policy, Serg," I say, taking the note from him. "Thank you."

Johnny's phone number was scrawled inside.

"Santi, venga," Valeria urges. "Please, let us go!"

"Buenas noches, Serg!"

He smiles and waves after us as we enter the elevator.

"You shouldn't have called Skywalker's mother a bitch," I reprimand Valeria on our ride up. "She may well be a very pleasant woman."

I had just enough time to finish this little lecture before she grabs me and kisses me with her tongue, telling me I was in for one passionate night.

And yes, folks, it was a good night indeed. So, I actually wound up staying in after all!

The following afternoon, I call Johnny's room, and a housekeeper informs me the guest has checked out. I try his cell phone instead, and a recorded message informs me the number is no longer in service.

"Perfect, Rico," I sigh. "Now what am I supposed to do with this gun?"

"What gun?" Valeria asks.

Nos vemos, Johnny Rico!

Acknowledgments

The Twice Killed Cat, Johnny Rico and El Oso Rojo, Luck of the I Wish, and Where in the World is Johnny Rico previously appeared in *Stray Dogs and Deuces Wild* (Horror Sleaze Trash Press, 2020).

Who Doesn't Like Strawberries and God Might Be a Woman previously appeared in *Quicksand Highway* (Horror Sleaze Trash Press, 2021).

Los Dos Chiflados, Psychopath Merit Badge, The Bare Necessities, and Johnny's Junk in the Trunk previously appeared in *Fingers in the Fan* Publisher (Impspired Press, 2022).

About the Author

The Odyssey of Judge Santiago Burdon began in the "City of Big Shoulders," as Sandburg called it in his poem "Chicago." He was born during Mayor Richard Daley's first days in office and Eisenhower's first term as President.

His father named him Judge, hoping he would pursue a career in law. He had no idea his son would end up appearing in front of so many.

Santiago attended Universities in the United States and abroad, focusing his studies on Victorian Literature and Authors. His short stories and poems have been featured in over two hundred magazines, on-line literary journals, podcasts, and anthologies. He was recognized in *Who's Who of Emerging Writers 2020* and again in 2021.

Previous Works

Stray Dogs and Deuces Wild: Cautionary Tales; Arthur Graham, Editor (Horror Sleaze Trash Press, 2020) – Burdon's first collection of 12 adventures featuring Santiago and Johnny Rico.

Not Real Poetry; Steve Cawte, Editor (Impspired Press, 2021) – A collection of 16 gritty poems. A sophisticated slap-in-the-face that will make you clear your throat and shift your weight from one side to another. Burdon does not waste words in an attempt to make you comfortable.

Quicksand Highway; Arthur Graham, Editor (Horror Sleaze Trash Press, 2021) – A collection of tales from skid row, bars, motels, and hospitals recounting drug running, bullet dodging, drug addiction, broken romance, and life in the fast lane. Extremely funny and always gritty.

Fingers in the Fan; Steve Cawte, Editor/Publisher (Impspired Press, 2022) - Another odyssey of Santiago, a recovering addict, ex-con, womanizer, gambler, and ill-fated pilgrim, along with his ex-cellmate, loose cannon, alcohol and drug fueled, Colombian carnal, Johnny Rico. While working as drug smugglers for a Mexican Cartel, the two encounter situations of structured devastation. This collection of short stories is filled with the same gritty dialogue, dark humor, and adventurous mayhem one comes to expect from Burdon.

Tequila's Bad Advice - Poetry with the Worm; Paul Gilliland, Editor/Publisher (Southern Arizona Press, 2023) – Burdon's second poetic collection containing 38 poems that will make you fall in love with his writing all over again as he twists your emotions between humor, fear, anxiety, joy, and devastation.

www.ingramcontent.com/pod-product-compliance
Lightning Source LLC
Chambersburg PA
CBHW061209170626
46809CB00003B/1300